Home for Love

An Adult Romance Novel

By Aneesa Price

Edited by Mary-Nancy's Eagle-Eye Editing

Praise for Coffin Girls by Aneesa Price

"Coffin Girls is a fabulous beginning to what is going to be an excellent series and I can't recommend this book enough to anyone looking for a new read! I started this on Thursday night and finished Friday afternoon! It was so good I dreaded putting it away just so I could actually sleep!" ~ Reviewer, Carrie Perkins-Cunningham

"Oh the Coffin Girls are my new heroes! I absolutely loved this book. I loved the Bayou plantation setting, the characters, the storyline, the conclusion, and I am chomping at the bit for the next installment." ~ Reviewer, Denise

"This is simply one of those books you can't go wrong with. I am sure before book 2 comes I will re-read this again. It is just too good to put down!" ~ Reviewer, chel73

Praise for Finding Promise by Aneesa Price

"The plot and storyline was brilliantly strong throughout. There is something about this story that will appeal to all women no matter what their frame of mind or the current situation in life!!! This really was an exceptional read!" ~ Reviewer, Janie

"It is a romance, an adult romance at times... But one where the characters are human flawed and smart enough to know it. I loved the book for the fact that it is a real story. Not a romance disguised as a story. I can't wait to read more by this author." ~ Reviewer and blogger, Wandah Panda

"If you enjoy awesome, heartfelt love stories then this is the story for you! Mrs. Price knows how to keep you interested from the first page to the very last! I love the way you can get totally wrapped up in her stories and you find yourself right there next to her characters feeling what they are feeling! I can't wait for the next book in this series!" - Reviewer, blogger and editor, M-N Smith

Praise for Ghost & Lovers by Aneesa Price

"The physical acts of making love in Ghost & Lovers are written so well I reread them twice and may look at them again in the future." ~ Author and reviewer, Roy Murry

"A steamy erotic read, this book is like nothing else I've read. Well written with a very unique concept, this book will have you gripped just to see where it's leading. With the descriptive nature, your imagination won't need much help picturing the scenes." ~ Reviewer, Claire Taylor

Dedication

I do not write a single word without thoughts of my beautiful family - my husband and daughters, Aaliyah and Zarah, in mind. Thank you for your continuous support and inspiration.

This novel is further dedicated to the amazing readers and reviewers whom without I'd be a completely unknown author. Thank you for your encouragement and enthusiasm for my work. A special note of gratitude must be given to the members of my Facebook fan club and street team. I strive to remain yours in romance.

Acknowledgements

My sincere gratitude for the support to these authors whom I admire as a fan and consider as friends...

Heather Killough Walden
Rose Pressey
Morgan Kearns
Rosanna Leo
Rhonda Plumhoff
PT Macias
Zrinka Jelic
CR Everett
Kelley Grealis
AJ Lape

I was pleasantly surprised when I asked for 'street team' volunteers on my fan club wall and many promptly put up their hands. Thank you to these wonderful readers, reviewers and friends who so selfishly promote me.

Alisa Jenkins
April Alvey
Breanna Lou
Carmen Ramirez Sanchez
Carrie Fort
Claire Taylor
Crystal Trent Dotson
Jackie Cervantes
Janie Lucas
Jessica Baker-Bridgers
Kelley Grealis
Krista Pruitt-Wallace
Layla Darnell
Mark Mackey
Mary-Nancy Cody Smith
Melissa Williams Brown
Ronda Lynch
Roxana Woodward
Sherry Boroto Cain
Tiffeny Moore
Sandra Ó HAirmhí Woods

Chapter 1

The tiny Cessna jerked and swayed in the Alaskan winter sky, over glistening white glaciers and snow-swathed mountains. Bree leaned closer to see what her daughter was gasping at through the plane's window.

"That's Devil's Peak, the highest mountain close to the valley," Bree stated. "We should be home soon." The peak stood as sentinel of a range of mountains and rivers that surrounded the valley housing her hometown - Devil's Creek, Alaska.

"Denelly's bigger," Amber declared.

"Denali," Bree corrected.

"Yes, Granddad said that only people from outside Alaska call it Mount McKinley." Amber spoke reverently of her great-grandfather.

It was adorable and a blessing, given that they were moving in with her grandparents.

"You're such a clever girl." Smiling, Bree kissed the top of Amber's head at her confident, "uh-huh" response.

"That's sooooooo pretty." The extra vowels were awarded to a picturesque lake further ahead. "Is that the one grandpa said we can skate on?"

"No, but there's another one like that closer to town. We'll take you skating there." Weary of the anticipatory gleam in Amber's eyes, Bree quickly added, "But remember that you must always have a grown up with you when you go skating."

"I know, mom. We've already had this conservation." Amber's attempt to sound grown up failed, with her sweet voice.

"Conversation, honey," corrected Bree, again.

"Uh-huh. We've had this conversation." Amber self-assuredly confirmed, oblivious to her blip. "I can't wait to skate and snowshoe and ski and…"

Bree opportunistically used her daughter's current bout of verbal diarrhea to take a moment a breath. She'd loved growing up in Alaska. Everyday had seemed like an adventure in the land of the final frontier. She'd never envied the heroes and heroines of childhood tales because she had lived one of her own, right in her own backyard. That was one of the many reasons she was returning. The small town offered Amber freedom that was missing from their tiny apartment in Columbus.

But there was pain in Devil's Creek too. So many good memories had been sullied when she'd fallen pregnant after high school graduation. The co-contributor and her high school sweetheart, Todd Hunter, had gone from being her future to an Alaskan adventurer. He was often absent even when he was around, with his head in the mountains and icy seas instead of with her.

Her grandparents had told her that he'd settled down as a successful businessmen and community member. They'd made a point of filling her in on his life. She'd also been told that he was still unmarried, though she hastened to remind herself, that was not why she'd returned. Given that she'd kept Amber's existence a secret from him for the past six years, she doubted that he'd feel romantically inclined towards her. Besides, Amber needed a good, stable home. That excluded romance, wild or otherwise and there had been nothing tame about the passion she'd shared with Todd.

Bree pushed down her own emotional mayhem and focused on Amber's wonder-filled face. "There it is!" She took Amber's hand, pointing the soft, little fingers in the direction of the town. "Devil's Creek, where your great-grandma and grandpa live."

"And my dad," announced Amber.

"Yes and your dad." Brianna hastily looked at Crazy Tommy, who exchanged a knowing smile with her, indicating that his suspicions had been confirmed. Bree silently commended herself that she'd decided to get the confession done immediately. She had approached her return with strategy and planning that would impress an army general. She would move in swiftly, get the job done and retreat because Amber's parentage would be the hot topic of the town grapevine within an hour of their landing.

After a jerky landing, she subjected Amber to a thorough inspection, zipped up insulated jackets, and adorned them both with fur-lined hats and gloves. As glad as she was to plant her feet on solid ground, the arctic climate, which she hadn't felt for seven years, hit her, going right through her many layers of clothing and straight through to the bone.

She pulled Amber back, who was trying to race through the thick snow towards her great grandparents. "Amber, I know you're excited, honey, but you have to promise to stay with mommy. The snow is colder than it looks and I don't want you to get all wet." Seeing the thoughts of finding out for herself written all over her daughter's face, she hastily added, "If you get wet, we'll have to take you straight to the farm and you'll miss out on visiting the town. You don't want that, do you?"

A deceptively demure, "Okay," was Amber's response. Bree silently blessed the Saints of Bribe as they stepped through the terminal doors and into their new life.

Bree watched Amber skip along with her grandparents, merrily on their way to do Christmas shopping. Drawing in iced oxygen, she headed for the Todd's building. It was a modest, single story painted deep blue with white trim around the sills. Its name, "Wild Alaska, Adventures and Tours," wasn't very original, but she appreciated the cheeky pun in the strapline. "We'll show you a devil of a time," She imagined that it would intrigue adventure seeking tourists. Bold writing on the window indicated that they offered any outdoor activity within the Devil's peak area. It suited him. Todd had enjoyed the outdoors and his ties to the Native Alaskan community had equipped him with knowledge of the area that rangers took years to acquire. Realizing that she was dawdling outside in the freezing cold, she squared her shoulders and stepped inside.

The reception area was inviting with light green walls adorned with Native Alaskan art and spectacular panoramas of the area. Occasional chairs and a coffee table offered seating next to a display area boasting an assortment of active gear. Todd was on the phone at a desk. At the sight of him, a strange combination of feelings assaulted her. Although she'd mentally prepared to see him, the familiar jolt of old feelings shot through her, along with a heightened sense of anxiety at what was about to unfold. Glancing around the room, she spotted what looked like a grown up Ella at reception.

She'd have to be friendly and play a good game until she could speak to Todd privately. As tempting as it was to get it over with, she couldn't exactly storm in and blurt out, "Hi Todd, Happy Father's Day!" So, instead, she greeted Ella.

"Hi," Ella responded, her brown eyes popping as flashes of recognition passed over her pixie face. "Bree Ramsay, welcome back. I heard about your parents, I'm really sorry."

The empathy she saw in Ella's eyes was the last thing she needed with her already turbulent emotions barely in check. She felt her eyes moisten and blinked rapidly. "Thanks Ella," she mumbled. "I've actually moved back now. I need to be with my grandparents for a while. How are you? Do you work here?"

"Uh-huh. I hit a rough patch after graduating high school and well," Ella waved a tattooed hand dismissively, "Todd gave me a job and has been helping me straighten out."

"I'm glad things are working out for you," Bree nodded, pasting a smile on her face. "And speaking of Todd, I was hoping to say hi." Still on the phone, he hadn't noticed her yet.

"Is he available afterwards?" Bree inquired. A part of her wanted Ella to say no and another desperately wanted him to be free so that she could get the inevitable confession over with.

"Sure. Why don't you have a seat?" Ella indicated the chairs. "He should be done soon."

Todd hung up the phone to see who Ella was talking to. What he saw made him choke on his coffee, drawing her attention to him. He couldn't believe that he was seeing Bree - the one that had left him and taken his heart with her. Time may have healed those wounds, but it didn't make him a monk - a point brought home swiftly as he felt the familiar stirrings of desire, a siren that always went off when she was around. He still felt the irresistible urge to run his fingers through her honey blonde mane and devour those curved, cherry reds, though he hadn't seen her in seven years.

Failing to take a slower gulp, he choked again when the scorching drink went down the wrong pipe. After an embarrassing fit of coughing, he stood up and looked straight into her eyes; blue ones that sparkled like a lake in summer and apparently, still had him acting like a fool.

"Hey, Bree. This is a nice surprise. What brings you back to town?" The smile curving his lips didn't quite reach his weary eyes.

"I've moved back after, you know, what happened to my folks." Accepting his condolences with the usual words, she pushed on, "I have to chat to you about something Todd. Is there somewhere private we can talk?"

Puzzled, but noticing Ella tampering with a nearby display, physically leaning towards them to improve the quality of her eavesdropping, he couldn't question her request for privacy. "Sure, there's a kitchen at the back," he offered. "We can chat there, have some coffee."

Despite the pending confession, Bree felt a frisson of attraction rekindle. She'd always had a penchant for his dark looks; slick black hair and chocolate eyes with a bone structure and sculpted body to taunt the most sainted woman. But looking at him was like looking at their daughter. Thoughts of Amber and the eminent discussion pulled her back to reality.

"Coffee would be great thanks," Bree responded. "I like what you did with the place." She waved a hand around on her way to the kitchen.

"Thanks, I'm happy with what I've done here," Todd replied in short, still confused.

Seating herself at the kitchen table, she accepted the mug of coffee and took a sip. He made it just the way she liked it strange how he remembered that little detail. "I can't believe how much the town has grown." The small talk was helping her build confidence. "How are Nick and Amy?" she asked after his younger siblings.

"They're doing well. Amy's studying marine biology out in Fairbanks and Nick's in Boston doing his articles." Justified pride filled his face. From what she recalled of his parents, she imagined that he'd put his siblings through college and was largely responsible for where they were today.

"That's great," she stated. Though genuinely pleased for them, anxiety was gnawing at her.

"So, Bree," asked Todd, "what did you want to chat about?"

"I left Devil's Peak because I thought it was over between us." She began with the explanation before giving him the news, hoping it would enable him to understand the why of it. "You'd left to go and fetch your dad when he died in Ketchikan. Then when you came back for the funeral I saw little of you. After you left to make your fortune crab fishing in Ketchikan, I just didn't hear from you. Not a word for four months."

"You know my mom wasn't capable of looking after us," Todd sounded weary. I had to go into crab fishing. It wasn't great work but it paid well and my family needed the money. I didn't call you because we were out at sea and when we got to shore I was usually too tired to do anything, but sleep."

"I realized that then," Bree, responded, "and I hung around waiting for you but you stayed there and I still didn't hear from you. I thought that you'd lost interest in us."

He ran his fingers through his hair, a sign she recognized as his way of biding time while he worked something out in conversation. "Why are you bringing this up now? It was a long time ago. I think we've both probably changed a lot from then. I thought this was a friendly visit to say hi." His tone had become defensive.

She closed her eyes for a short moment and took a deep breath before continuing. "I got pregnant the last time we were together, after the funeral. I wanted to tell you, but I didn't know what was going on or how to reach you."

He flinched, guilt overwhelming him. "I'm sorry, Bree. I'm sorry you had to go through that and lose the baby without me being there for you." He ran his fingers through his hair again. "If I'd known I would've pulled myself together and come to you. I didn't come back after fishing season because I got a job in a canning factory and took it because I needed the money. It was long hours and I wasn't in a good space. My life wasn't playing out the way I hoped it would."

Eyes reflecting remorse, he continued, "I took you for granted. I took it for granted that you'd be here when I got back. I know we spoke of marriage and a future together, but at that point I didn't know what future I had for myself or if I could help give my brother and sister a future, if I could look after my mom. I didn't dare think that I could look after you too. I came back shortly after that, but you were gone already. I'd lost so much - my dad, my dreams, the hopes I had for our future. I didn't believe in myself then yet, so I took your leaving as confirmation that you wanted better things."

"Wait," Bree interjected, tears escaping slowly. "I didn't lose the baby Todd. I had our daughter, Amber. We've just moved to Devil's Creek."

"What?" he asked, looking as though she sucker-punched him. "I don't think I heard that correctly, Bree."

"I didn't lose the baby." She recoiled at his shock. She'd told herself to expect this, but nothing would have prepared her for the reality.

"I'm sorry. I was young, I didn't know what was going on with you, and then when I told my folks, they were furious. I didn't know what to do, so I did what they asked me to do." She drew in a breath. "They told me that we were moving to Columbus. My dad had been toying with the idea of accepting a job offer there and they saw it as the perfect opportunity for us to get away, for me to start fresh." Bree wept openly, equally consumed by relief and guilt.

"She must be over six years old then?" His voice was vibrating with contained anger.

"Yes," She nodded, barely audible

"Then why the hell didn't you tell me sooner?" he roared.

Hunting for a tissue from her handbag, she continued, "I was a pregnant teenager, confused and relocating to another state. I got through things first a day at a time and then a month at a time. I was studying, taking care of her and working part-time, because I no longer lived with my parents. And, then the longer I kept it from you, the harder it was to tell you, because the more afraid I became of your reaction." She rambled, barely taking a breath between words

"Okay." He interrupted her. "I get it. It was tough. But, you only have yourself to blame. Sure, I can understand that you kept it from me when I was going through a rough patch, but that didn't last. I would have helped you; you didn't need to go through it alone. In fact, it is my duty and my right to have helped take care of our daughter. Your grandparents must've told you that I'd cleaned up and was doing okay. "

"I'd heard that from them. You're right, but my parents kept telling me differently. They said that you wouldn't want to be bogged down with a child that you'd never wanted and reminded me of how you'd left after the funeral. I didn't know what to do." She was pleading for understanding now. "I'm sorry," she reiterated, despite her knowing that it didn't help. "I know it's not a good enough reason, but I did what I thought was right for Amber at the time."

"Okay, just give me a moment. I can't think right now." He walked to the windows and looked out at the street at the back of the building. The Brown kids' were snow-shoeing in the front yard, yelling at each other in excitement. Zack Brown was six. He knew that because he'd seen the party out on the front lawn the previous summer, a big helium balloon that had proudly displayed his age. Zack was his daughter's age Amber's age. It felt odd, alien. He had a daughter. Holy crap! Family was important to him and not knowing his daughter was a living nightmare! As much as he wanted to shake Bree, he had to focus on Amber.

"Okay," he repeated, returning to sit at the table again. "I want to be angry at you. I am angry at you. I've missed the first six years of my daughter's life. I've missed your pregnancy, watching her grow inside you. I've missed doctor's appointments and those scan things. I've missed birthdays and Christmases. I have a daughter who I don't know and who doesn't know me. Nothing can ever get that back for me or for her. That's lost now." It made him sick to think of it.

"I know. I'm..." Bree began.

He interrupted her apology, "No, you don't know. You couldn't know. You've stolen that from me. I can forgive you for not telling me straight away. I admit that I was a mess after my dad died. I can't forgive the past few years when you'd heard that I was here and that I was okay. That is inexcusable."

"I would feel the same way if I were you."

The simple statement gave him pause. Raising his brows at that, he asked, "What made you change your mind?"

"After my parents died in the crash, my grandparents came for the funeral and spoke to me about you. They'd tried to do so before, but my parents had always run interference. They made me realize that it wasn't too late to tell you about Amber…" She broke off, breathed in and started again, "I also wanted to give Amber a home, family and the roots she's begun to crave. I've told you because of Amber. Everything I've done since I left here has been for her. I know it wasn't right, what I've done, but I did it only because I thought it was best for her. I thought I knew you and when you acted the way you did after your dad died, I felt as though I didn't know you at all. It disillusioned me and I didn't know what to believe about what I was hearing about you, so I carried on and tried to do what I thought was best for her. I did do my best for her." Her voice held conviction now. "No matter what you think of me now, I can guarantee you that I raised our daughter well, with love, with care, and all that I am. I gave all of me the last few years to her and she's wonderful because of it."

"The Bree I loved would have done that, so I can believe that you raised her well, but the Bree I knew would also not have kept this from me." He tried to focus on reasoning and bank the hurt and anger. He needed to move forward. He needed to see his daughter, get to know her. "Okay, let's focus on Amber. I guess she's with your grandparents?" At her nod, he urged, "Tell me about her."

She spent the next half hour telling him more about Amber, seeing betrayal and hurt move towards pride and anticipation. "What do you want to do? She's at the diner."

"I feel like racing across there and grabbing her. I need to meet her. But, I don't want to do it in the diner and stir up gossip; that'll make things harder for her. I'll follow you to the farm. Does she know about me?"

"Yes," replied Bree. "She knows your name and what you look like from pictures we took together in high school. My parents thought I'd gotten rid of it all, but I kept them."

"How did you explain my absence?" Todd hated that his daughter might think he'd been as neglectful a father as his own had been. He couldn't fight back the tears and mopped roughly at them while they slid down his cheeks.

"At first I told her that Alaska was far away and that was why she didn't get to see you and her great-grandparents. She's a bright kid, though and I knew that when we moved back that the explanation wasn't enough, so I gave her a child appropriate version of the events. She knows that I was scared to tell you because I wasn't sure of what your reaction would be or what you'd be like after all these years. I've told her that I was wrong and more importantly, she knows that you didn't know that she was around. I took the blame for it and rightly so."

She stopped and saw the remark he was about to make. "Yes. I know that it didn't have to be that way. The fact is that now we are in this situation and as much as I can imagine that you hate me for what I did, we have a beautiful daughter and I want to do what's best for her. I want us to work together to raise her. I've asked her and she wants to give it a try."

"I'm her dad. She shouldn't have to give it a try," Todd scoffed.

"I imagine that it feels that way, but try to imagine what it feels like for her," Bree interjected. "She's just six, Todd. Even though I've lied to her and to you, she got over her initial anger at me because I'm her mother and I'm a good mother. I've worked very hard at it. So, it's natural that she'd forgive me." She looked him squarely in the eye now, ignoring the guilt coursing through her. "But, she doesn't know you. That's going to take time. Todd, I do blame myself for the current situation and I'm sorry for the pain I've caused you and confusion she'll be going through. But, she's smart and loved and she'll cope if we handle this well."

Interpreting his nod as encouragement, she continued, "I'm not asking you to forgive me. I wouldn't be callous enough to expect that, but I'm asking you to work with me."

"She's my daughter and I want what's best for her too." His voice held a hint of steel. "I won't," he corrected "I can't forgive you yet, but with my family background, you should know that I wouldn't allow my feelings for you to impact my child."

"Thank you," Bree whispered and got up to leave. "We arrived in Devil's Peak just before I came over. I have to go and get Amber settled in at the farm. Tonight, when she's asleep, we can work out the next steps?"

"I can do that," Todd nodded, sounding and acting far too civil for the emotions assaulting him. "I'll get things sorted out here and meet you at the farm in an hour's time."

Bree nodded, then turned around and walked towards the diner, ambivalent of her surroundings. She wasn't worried about him meeting Amber. She'd meant what she'd said; her daughter was good, strong and had loved ones ready to support her. Bree walked in a daze, because she realized that she'd wronged the one man she'd loved in her life.

Chapter 2

Todd pulled his truck into the Ramsay Farm's driveway. Daniel's truck was in front of the house, indicating that they were all inside – including his unknown daughter. Taking a deep breath, Todd took a moment and looked around. If his daughter had inherited his love of the outdoors, she'd thrive on the farm. The farmhouse was a beautiful wooden, A-frame structure adorned with a multitude of windows, which overlooked four hundred and eighty acres of central Alaskan forest and farmland. Currently there was no visible view the long winter night had plunged everything into darkness and the only indication of light was the soft yellow glow coming from the windows and the outdoor lighting around the various farm buildings.

The Ramsay family had been amongst the first non-Native people to come to this area along with the hundreds of prospectors during the gold rush. Unlike the rest of the fortune seeking pioneers, the Ramsay's had come to farm. Daniel's parents had bought the land, which had been nothing, more than virgin forest, from the government in the hopes that they could apply their knowledge of harsh Irish climates to successfully farm Alaskan ground. Ireland, however, had been insufficient preparation for the extremities and remoteness of Alaska and they'd had to supplement their income with the establishment of a roadhouse, servicing the prospectors in the gold rush while stubbornly working at farming. Daniel and Moira carried on the legacy and were a big part of both the Devil's Peak farming community and the town at large. They had a nice operation, an eclectic mix of dairy and crop farming. Like most rural

Alaskans, they subsidized their income with a variety of ventures. They also grew vegetables and kept a few chicken coops for eggs.

Looking around, he spotted the well restored and maintained roadhouse that was now part of the historical tour of Devil's Peak. Todd didn't often get requests to include that in his tours, being mostly focused on adventures, but one or two slipped in now and again during the tourist season. The Ramsay's also gave farm tours to school children to help create awareness of early agriculture in Alaska. It sure beat reading about it in books. That was how he'd first met Bree - a tour of the farm during Elementary school. They'd fast become friends and later began dating. The farm had often served as his sanctuary when he'd needed to get away from the troubles at home. This made the farm as familiar to him as his own home.

Grabbing the big, oversized stuffed toy, he made his way to the front door. He'd made a quick stop at Suzy's gift shop, deciding that he had a lot of birthdays to make up for and that he may as well start now. It was a moose that had a sweater with yellow and red writing announcing, "Welcome to Alaska." He'd also bought her a card and the act of signing it, "love Dad," had been a surreal experience.

It hadn't quite sunk in yet that he was a father. He studied his reflection in the car window and noted that nothing was different. He still looked the same, was the same and yet, everything had changed. If someone had told him this morning that he'd be visiting the Ramsay Farm to spend time with his daughter, he'd have thought that they were nuts. He didn't doubt that she was his, though. Her age, Bree's disappearance and the glimpse of her he'd caught as she had gotten into Daniel's truck earlier had been enough to make all the pieces fall into place. After he'd seen Amber, he'd called his brother and sister, who'd both been more delighted than shocked. They had always loved Bree and there had been many uncomfortable arguments with them when she'd left as they pushed for him to go after her and he'd steadfastly refused.

"Hi." Bree called from the front porch. "Come on up." The greeting left Todd feeling more unhinged – it was just too bizarre because the way she greeted him hit again and took him straight back to high school. It was odd, given their earlier conversation, though Todd acknowledged this by the too bright smile she displayed, that she was probably over-compensating for nervousness.

"Thanks," he dipped his head in greeting. "Are your grandparents around?"

"Yep," Bree replied. "Gran and I are just finishing up with the cooking so you're just in time. Granddad and Amber have been tasked with setting the table." She stopped in the arctic entry, meant to help keep the cold at bay, and waited for him to shed the layers he wore. She pointed at the stuffed toy, her anxiety betrayed by a slight tremor in her hand. "That is very sweet of you. She'll like it. Thank you."

He shrugged dismissively. "I didn't know what to get and went for the safe bet, I guess. Suzy's questions about girly girl or active type threw me."

Lips curving, she let a laugh slip out, "She's a bit of both, but this is just fine and very apt. Let's go so you can give it to her. She's as anxious to meet you as I'm sure, you are."

Feeling relieved that he'd gotten it right, he followed her into the dining room and was hit by an emotional lightning bolt. "She looks just like me," he whispered in awe. His daughter giggled at her grandfather who was tickling her while she lay half-suspended over his shoulder. Amber was beautiful, the inheritance of his bone structure was softened a bit by an indescribable something that she must have gotten from her petite mother.

Sensing his cautiousness, Bree took his hand in hers, making him jerk in surprise. She duly ignored it and pulled him towards Amber and her granddad. Through the shock, he recognized that Bree still had the ability to sync with what he was feeling and give him what he needed - silent encouragement. Then again, he mentally shrugged; Bree's eagerness could also be attributed to her wanting to get this uncomfortable introduction over with.

Their approach cut through Daniel and Amber's absorption with each other. "Todd, nice to see you boy. Welcome," Daniel boomed. He ruffled Amber's hair eye's twinkling appreciatively at her protests when her bangs got into her eyes.

Todd took the hand that Daniel offered, glad of something familiar, and went through the ritual pleasantries. All the while, his eyes kept darting to Amber, she had eyes like his, and they stared at him unnervingly as she stood ramrod straight next to her mom.

"I couldn't wait to meet Amber," Todd said aloud. He approached her cautiously and crouched so that they were level. "In fact," he said to all of them, "I've arranged things so that I have more time off during the school break, so that we can spend some time together. I also thought that I could help you get settled, Amber, Bree."

Todd went over to Amber and kneeled down like he would with a hurt animal he was rescuing from the wild, thinking that it would seem less threatening. He held out his hand, as a hug and kiss seemed a bit premature and looked at her directly, gently. "Hi Amber, I'm really happy to meet you."

When Amber continued to stare wordlessly at him, he felt the trickle of anxiety within him rapidly begin to grow. His time in the wild had taught him patience though, so he kept his gaze soft and steady as he mentally banked down his apprehension.

"Daddy?" Amber's voice quivered. "Are you my dad?"

"Sure am." Todd replied, taking her little hand in his big one, fighting the urge to sweep her into his arms. "I'm really sorry I've never had the opportunity to meet you before, but I promise you that if it's what you want, I'll make it up to you, starting now. Would you like that?"

Nodding shyly. Amber replied, "I've always wanted a daddy." Tilting her head, she looked questioningly at him, "Mom said that I look like you." With relief and a watery smile, he noted that Amber's curiosity was winning the battle over other emotions she might be feeling.

The first hurdle had been crossed, Todd thought. Fighting the urge to whoop in relief, he let his lips curve widely. He looked up at Bree who was trying, but failing miserably at wiping her tears discreetly. A tentative unit, the three of them stood alone in the quiet of the dining room. Daniel had quietly slipped away, leaving the three of them to move into their new life in privacy.

"She's right," Todd, responded to Amber, "Do you want to see?" He held out his arms to her, praying that she'd come. When she did, he used the opportunity to put his face to her neck and breathe in her smell. And just like that, the bond was formed. The feeling to nurture and protect was overwhelming. Keeping things light so that he didn't scare Amber, he approached the big decorative mirror that hung above the side-server. Her resemblance to him was even more startling as they looked into the mirror with her little face next to his.

"Now, what do you think we have that's the same?" Todd ventured, looking at Amber in the reflection.

"I don't have gold hair or blue eyes like mom," Amber stated while thoughtfully examining their images in the mirror. "Mine are like yours."

"That's right." He risked it and kissed the top of her head, encouraged yet again, when she didn't back away. He gently touched her pert little chin and then pointed to his own. "But you got your chin from your mom."

"Mom, can you come here please?" Amber called out, so that Bree could stand next to them and look in the mirror too. "I do get that from mom," Amber agreed, fascinatedly. "So, I have something from both of you." Amber's tone was satisfied and her gaze content.

Bree took all of this in and looked at the three of them. No matter what, they were a family and they were together at this moment. Meeting Todd's eyes in the mirror, she saw the same determination to make things work in his expression. She nodded her agreement, silently understanding that they'd come to a truce for now. "Thank you." She mouthed, acknowledging his concession.

XXX

Todd was sitting on the porch, watching the spectacular show afforded by the Northern Lights as the green, white, and red streams of light tangoed in the blackened sky. The sight prompted him to philosophically reflect on the bigger picture, which was that his newfound family was part of a greater universe, a greater plan. He needed to anchor the day's events to something and he figured that thinking of it in the greater scheme of things might just help, just as the beer that he was nursing was helping him settle. Sipping slowly, thinking even slower, he reviewed the day's events.

Amber was wonderful. Within minutes, no seconds, she'd tugged him in all the right places and put a tag on him that claimed him as hers, instead of the other way around, as parents are want to do. He'd had many firsts that night - first knowledge and sight, first interaction with his daughter, first dinner and first bath and first bedtime story. He'd been unequivocally pleased when she'd requested a kiss and hug goodnight – another first.

He'd always expected that he'd be a father one day but just hadn't settled with the right woman. Hell, he'd had the right woman, but she'd gone and left him seven years ago without telling him she was pregnant. In the silence offered by the unoccupied porch, the cover of darkness aiding it, he could acknowledge the bitterness he felt at the loss of the years he could've had with Amber and that it was eating at him. He'd had enough bitterness growing up. His dad hadn't been around and had left him and his siblings with a mother that was self-absorbed and incapable of looking after them, so he had to step in and be mother and father to both his siblings and himself. Then along had come Bree. Bree had breathed new life and hope into him. She'd shown him another side of love, of belonging, innocent fun, and acceptance. Being exposed to her family, as intimately as he'd been, coming to this farm for dinners, Sunday lunch, and just to hang around had proven that there was normalcy out there and not just on TV.

It had been great until his father had died and crumbling under the weight of the financial responsibility and the demands required by his family, he'd caved and gotten as snowed under as the land in winter. So, he understood why she refrained from confiding in him initially. He also understood why her parents and grandparents had kept it from him too and didn't encourage her to involve him in her life. But, he couldn't understand why they remained secretive when they knew that he'd cleaned up. Why it took her parents' death to make her come back and start involving him in their daughter's life was hard to fathom. He looked out into the dark and acknowledged the anger that he felt towards Bree, Daniel, and Moira. He'd been to the farm many times. How could they greet him, make small talk with him, discuss business, and keep such a secret? Anger bubbled, belied by his still form.

"It's a cold night for a man to be pondering out on a porch." The lyrical rumble of Daniel's voice reached out to him, a white flag calling a truce. "Then again, that man must have had quite a day to do such sitting." The wooden bench creaked as Daniel sat on the opposite end.

"You could say that," Todd answered, wanting suddenly to wring the old man's neck.

"I imagine that you have some questions for me, Todd," Daniel's expression was wary, remorseful. "And I'm offering explanations. You're entitled."

"Funny that you say that, Daniel," Todd couldn't keep the bitterness out of his voice, spitting the other man's name out like a filthy word. "I was just sitting here and thinking how you could look me in the eye all these years, call me a friend, and lie to me"

"I acknowledge that we lied to you," a feminine voice replied. Moira joined them, and shook her head at the seat that Daniel offered, pulling over a chair to sit right next to Todd. It never paid to show a man that you were intimidated or weary of him, no matter the circumstances. "I had my part in it too and I'll take the blame along with my Daniel." Moira took a breath and continued, "For what it's worth, we're sorry. But it was neither our tale nor our secret to tell. All we could do was try to talk some sense into our son and granddaughter. And we did that, every chance we could. Even when we mourned the passing of our child, we thought of you, Amber and Bree. It was hard to lie to you, to 'look you in the eye' as you say, but we didn't know what else to do."

"It's hard being a parent, Todd, and when you're a grandparent, you're not necessarily less involved emotionally, just less mandated to be involved." Daniel interjected. "You raise kids, being participants in every aspect of their lives only to have to butt out when they think they're old enough."

Noting that Daniel sounded weary and old, so like his age but unlike his character, Todd allowed for some of what they said to register. He felt older, wearier too and could only manage a nod at them in response.

Taking that as encouragement, Daniel carried on. "Then your grandkids come along. For us, that was Bree. Because they lived with us, she was ours in more ways than just a grandkid. But, when she got pregnant, things changed in this household. The arguments we had with Bree's mother and our son were fiery." Daniel's voice found surer footing. "We never agreed with the way they wanted to deal with the pregnancy or with how they treated Bree."

"How did they treat Bree?" Todd inquired.

Moira answered, "They made living with them unbearable, punishing her - not physically, but emotionally - for what they saw as betrayal of the values they'd raised her by."

"I can imagine that it can't be easy finding out that your teenage daughter is pregnant. So it was probably just shock and disappointment," Todd's tone and the wave of his hand were dismissive.

Moira tried another angle. "Todd, do you remember what it was like with your mom and dad?"

"What's that got to do with anything?" Todd's bark was defensive; they were tiring him out.

"Now, now, don't get yourself into a twist," Moira replied, "I'm just trying to paint the picture for you."

Moira continued, urged by his silence. "Well, it was pretty much like that for her too. As soon as they left Alaska, they isolated themselves from her - she even gave birth to Amber on her own and we only found out afterwards. When she was discharged from the hospital, she took a taxi home with her new baby and found an empty house because her parents had gone to work. They were self-absorbed, more concerned with their disappointment and how the pregnancy would affect the esteem of others. They punished her by neither showing her love nor giving her financial support. She was a young mother fresh out of high school and working any job, she could get where she could also look after the baby, while trying to study to create a better future. Her parents were not rich, but they were comfortable enough that they could've helped her out." Moira had to stop when she no longer could keep her tears at bay, feeling the pain of knowing that someone she loved dearly had suffered and that she'd been unable to help.

Handing her a handkerchief from his pocket, Daniel took over, observing that some of the steam the boy had been bottling up had begun to dissipate. "We found out about things after the first summer we went down to see Amber. Bree had moved out and was living in a shoebox that served as bedroom, nursery, kitchen, and bathroom. It wasn't in the best of places and it makes me angry to think of it, but there was hardly a thing to eat in the place. Our Bree was raised right so the place was clean, but it's easy to keep a place clean that has nothing in it. Bree was sleeping on a couch someone had thrown out and had Amber in a cheap cot that she'd scrimped and saved for. The fanciest thing she owned was the laptop we gave her when she graduated from high school and she used that 3G business we bought as well so that she could do her studies online to become a teacher. She didn't tell us what was going on, because she was afraid that we'd treat her the way her parents had." Daniel felt his own eyes moisten and silent tears, revoked by past pain, slipped slowly down his weather-worn cheeks.

"We do okay, Todd," Daniel said, wiping the tears away roughly with his hand. "You know that. Life in Alaska is hard and chews up the money as fast as you make it if you farm, but we'd managed to save a bit. So, we cashed that in and used our time in Columbus to set Amber up. We got her a better place, not fancy, but safer, a bit bigger, and some basic furniture. We paid for her studies and put a bit of money every month in her bank account, so that she could buy some food, some things for the baby and so on. She's a good girl and we trusted her and she hasn't let us down. Yes, she could've told you about Amber sooner and yes, we spoke to her about it often, but the poor girl was going through so much with her own parents and trying to get by that we couldn't press. We were scared that she'd cut us off and of what would happen if she did. She was like a deer caught in the headlights and we were too scared to make a move, so we did what we could."

Moira moved to sit in between the two men, taking a hand of each man in one of hers. "Todd, we never saw our son again until his funeral – we were that disappointed in him. The first time we went to see Amber and saw what they'd done, we were so angry that we went straight to them and had a very, very unpleasant argument." Shutting her eyes, she pushed the memory away before she carried on. "The next time I saw the boy I bore unto this earth was when he was put into the grave. So, things aren't as simple as they seem."

Todd wasn't made of ice and he knew what it was like to see someone you loved, someone who disappointed you once they'd gone from the earth. He wiped the tears from his own face and tugged at their linked hands until he had her wrapped in his arms, patting her back as she sobbed and grieved. Over her head, his eyes met Daniel's moist ones. "I think that there's been enough dwelling in the past and enough blame to go around for all of us." Gently pushing Moira away, he cradled her face in his hands and kissed her on the cheek. "I'm sorry you had to go through that again to give me my answers, but I'm glad you did because it helped me put things into perspective. Thank you."

With a teary smile, Moira responded, "Then it's been worth it. You are a fine man, Todd."

Daniel threw a smile at the woman of his heart and then a serious expression at Todd. "So, what is this perspective you've gotten?" He looked questioningly at Todd. His voice held a firmness that hinted at protectiveness. "Todd, as much as we want to do what's right for you and Amber, we can't let it be at the expense of Bree's happiness. She's been through too much already." Daniel's voice held warning.

"I get that now. I don't want to hurt Bree." Todd ran his fingers through his hair, his habitual act when thinking or frustrated. "I won't deny that I'm still hurt and angry at her for keeping things from me. I would've helped her. But," he continued, before Daniel and Moira could interject and get defensive, "I do know what it is like to have to go it alone, without parents that don't do what they should. It doesn't lessen the hurt, the anger, but it does help me put a foot forward."

He met both of their gazes, "I want what's best for Amber and at the moment, that means stability here in Devil's Peak with both of her parents and her great-grandparents. The plain truth is that if Bree's unhappy, being the only sure thing that Amber's had in her life, it will make Amber unhappy, and I don't want that. I realise that Bree and I have to work together, and seeing as we're being frank, I'll share with you that she and I came to that agreement earlier today when she told me about Amber."

"That's a perspective that we can live with." Daniel breathed a sigh of relief. "I'll repeat what I said at dinner. You're welcome here anytime and we'll do our bit to help you kids - whatever it takes to make this work"

"Thank you," Todd shook Daniel's hand in the age-old masculine gesture of understanding.

Daniel sat back in his chair and lit his pipe, puffing in satisfaction born out of resting after an eventful day, "So what's next?"

"What's next is that I take my first vacation from work and spend it with my daughter and her mother. I'll help them settle in and show Amber a bit of Alaska. I'll take things one day at a time. Speaking of day, the winter one's are short and I wanted to discuss Bree's plans with her so that we can work out an itinerary of sorts. I don't know much yet about being a dad, but I can do an itinerary." God knows he does enough of them for work; he can do a super one for his daughter. He'd show her the best of Alaska that he could. "And speaking of Bree, where is she?"

Daniel looked at him sheepishly, "Bree's fast asleep in Amber's room. She read another bedtime story after you kissed Amber goodnight and couldn't keep her eyes open. The poor girl's worn out from the trip."

Aah… Todd caught on, "And that created the perfect opportunity for the two of you to corner me."

"Well, you know we meant well," said Moira the guilt of the naughty etched in her blush. "And we're old; we can't wait for you young people to catch on to things properly. I need to see things put right before I meet my maker."

"That's bull, Moira. Old, yeah right!" Todd let out a laugh and joined in by both Moira and Daniel, let it roll. "Using your age when I know that you can do most things better than younger folk is just downright manipulative. Meet your maker. Huh!" It felt good to laugh after the day he'd had and he let it go. Moira and Daniel must've felt the same because before long, the three of them were wiping at tears again, but this time, the tears were born of laughter and relief.

Chapter 3

The next morning Todd visited the Ramsay farm because it felt odd to have met his six year old daughter the day before and not see her upon waking up. Warming his hands on the coffee mug, he bid farewell to Moira and Daniel who conspicuously found a long list of chores that were waiting for them outside on the farm-side of the property. Amber was still sleeping the exhausted sleep, born of experiencing too many emotions and change.

So, in the twilight haze that constituted the late Alaskan morning, Todd and Bree were alone in the large farmhouse kitchen. He elected not to tell her the details of the discussion he'd had with her grandparents. Intuitively, feeling that it would embarrass her, which was self-defeating. He'd lain awake for hours the previous night and had made the decision to do whatever it took to help Amber acclimate to her newly extended family and her new home, which meant working closely with Bree. He wanted to give Amber what he'd never had - an active mother and father, a warm home, and an integrated family. Although he had twisted the options, rung them out then twisted them again, the only feasible option seemed to be marriage. To his mind, that was the first step towards attaining stability. Of course, he was still furious with Bree, but he had to put those feelings aside for the sake of his daughter. He'd loved Bree once and perhaps in time, could forgive her and they could become friends again.

He couldn't deny that he was still attracted to her. Just looking at her sipping at the steamy liquid across the table had him panting internally and sent his thoughts into the gutter. In fact, the table held some interesting prospects if you added Bree and his imagination into the equation. So, it wouldn't be too much of a stretch to be married if it meant that he could see her every night and have Amber in his life full time. His own relationship with his part-time father had been tempestuous at best and he didn't want that for his own child.

He'd make the best of the cards he'd been dealt, but it was too soon to play his hand. She was still skittish and he had to woo her, play the game, and get to know Amber. The rest would follow. He was determined to walk away a winner.

"So, I was thinking that we could work out a schedule of sorts," Todd interrupted the silence. "That way, I can spend time with Amber and show her some of the sights and be involved in settling her in and preparing her for school. It might also give you some time to get settled; reacquaint yourself with the town and old friends. What do you think?"

Bree didn't really know what to think. She was dumbstruck by his lack of anger and eagerness to work together. Gone was the frosted reproach of the day before and what she'd supposed would be the biggest hurdle, had turned out to be a non-issue. Not wanting to look a gift horse in the mouth, she eagerly took the bait, "Sure that sounds great. In fact, it sounds perfect. I have already enrolled her and filled out all of the forms. Everything has been submitted." She stopped rambling and took a moment. "I'll be teaching at the school too as I'm taking over for Laura, who resigned to stay home and look after her baby."

"So, you're a teacher, huh?" He asked with genuine pleasure for her. He knew that she'd qualified as a teacher, but couldn't tell her without informing her of his confidential chat with her grandparents the previous evening. "Your studies have paid off then. I'm happy for and proud of you, Bree. Well done."

"Thanks." She was once again puzzled. What had brought on this change, first his decision to work amicably with her as a parent and now praise? "Things have worked out quite nicely. I start my first day at the pre-kindergarten class the day before Amber starts school. So, when she starts school, I'll be just across the playground if she needs me. I've also arranged a tour of the school for her, she will meet her new teacher, and the principal the day before school starts so it won't be so foreign to her. If you want, you could spend the morning with Amber and then bring her over to the school and be part of the tour and meetings?"

"Sounds good," Todd agreed. "What about in between then and now?"

"The only other plans I have are probably the same as yours so I don't see why we can't do it together. I have to do some Christmas shopping and I want to decorate the house with Amber and my grandparents. They've been putting it off until we got here so she could be part of it. It will be her first family Christmas with more than just her and me. In fact, why don't you join in? She can have both her parents with her and her great-grandparents." He nodded, wrote it down on the makeshift itinerary he'd created, so she carried on, "I also want to get her some warm clothes. Gran sent me some basics, but it's not enough."

"You might want to get some for yourself as well, I imagine," Todd stated, as he scribbled.

"Some what?" She looked at him questioningly.

"Clothes. You probably need some too?" Except for a change in shirt, she was wearing the same things she'd worn the day before. He ignored her gaping expression and spoke as he wrote, "Clothes for Amber and Bree. Okay, what's next?"

She flushed with embarrassment. "Todd, that's very sweet of you, but I can't afford that. I'll get some things for Amber. I've got what I need for myself. I'm good, thank you."

He waved away her protest. "With all due respect, Bree, you're the mother of my daughter and I'll be paying for Amber's clothes, so I can certainly spring for some stuff for you too." He cut off her counter-argument. "No, don't argue, you owe me, so indulge me please?" Geez, he remembered the Bree he used to go out with and how much time she'd spent grooming and primping with makeup, clothes, and shoes. She'd been just like the other girls and had spoken to him of clothes while he'd nodded, trying to score points while not understanding a word she'd said. That Bree was miles apart from the one sitting across from him who felt that one outfit and a few changes of a shirt was enough. Guilt tugged at him, but he shoved it away, focusing on wooing instead.

"You have a say in Amber's life, Todd, not mine. Don't play dirty." Her eyes were narrowed and a pink glow of irritation stained her beautiful face. She never could hide what she felt.

"Okay. Sorry. That was out of line." He deliberately reached out for her hand and ignored the frisson of excitement that the contact ignited. He offered an explanation. "You've been the sole provider for the last seven years. I should've been helping with that. So, to me, buying you some clothes and some other things you might need is self-indulgence. My way of making up for lost time and it helps with the guilt, knowing that I haven't contributed at all so far. So, please may I buy you some things?"

He put on the works. She'd never been able to resist him when he pleaded with her so reasonably in the past and it looked like she still couldn't resist. "Okay, fine. I'll accept the offer as long as it doesn't become a regular occurrence. That's sweet of you. Thank you."

"My pleasure," he grinned, thinking that he planned to make the upkeep of his family a very regular occurrence in his life. "Now, before we go wake up our sleeping beauty," he relished the feel of the word, our, on his tongue, "let's put some activities together on this list." He pointed to the piece of paper he'd been writing on.

xxx

The next few days went by in an activity-filled blur. They completed their shopping for Christmas, clothes, and school supplies by the second day on the infamous itinerary. This afforded the perfect opportunity for Amber and Bree to see the variety of new stores that had sprung up in the booming tourist town. Bree remembered having to fly to Fairbanks when she was growing up to go on a shopping spree. Although Fairbanks, being the closest metropolis to Devil's Peak, was not far in distance, the terrain between the town and the city constituted a web of rivers, mountains, forests, and vast, lonely expanses of uninhabited, wild land, so the most efficient way to get to the city was to fly. Fortunately, coordinated flights out of town, such as those provided by courier services, Todd's business being one of the providers, and the economic growth in Devil's Peak made that a superfluous exercise now. Bree, for one, was glad of that. The short daylight hours in winter meant that you crammed as much as you could in the little time provided and things done quickly and conveniently was a bonus.

Shopping in town also allowed them to fuel the rumors enough so that everyone could have a good yack about the ready-made family and get it out of their systems. The gossip was inevitable and putting it off would've only drawn it out. She wasn't naïve though. She knew that they'd soon expect a wedding invitation and the idea was sweet, but completely impractical. As much as she had loved him before, she was not going to jeopardize the hard-earned equilibrium in her life with romance.

Currently, things with Todd seemed to be going well, if a bit tentative. He spent every moment of his time with Amber and by default her too. When he wasn't showing them the sites in and around town, he spent time with Amber on the farm. Todd had even joined in the Christmas decorating activities, respectfully taking over the climbing and physically demanding tasks from Daniel. At Amber's insistence, his home had also becoming a kitsch, tinsel-twinkling zone of red, green, and gold.

Bree loved his home. It was a modest, ranch-style house on a good five acres of land, situated in a family-oriented neighborhood that skirted the edges of town. The house had enough room to build on or to just enjoy some of the outdoors in his backyard. Todd hadn't seen the point of decorating his house, not really being the Christmas celebrating type, but Amber had managed to manipulate him nicely. Bree let that one go, admittedly finding an immature sense of satisfaction in his grumpiness as he paid for a horde of unnecessary knick-knacks.

Bree was making rosemary and bread stuffing for the turkey when she heard Amber chattering as she ran into the kitchen, Todd and Daniel following her closely behind. "Gran, mom," Amber exclaimed, bobbing up and down in excitement. "I saw Santa and his house and these huge ice cupltures."

"Ice sculptures," Bree corrected. Amber had been treated with a trip to the North Pole, a town recreated in Alaska in honor of the Christmas spirit.

Amber nodded, "Uh-huh, and they were in all these really cool shapes. I saw Bambi, animals, and even elves. Then Dad and grandpa took me to have hot chocolate and waffles at Santa's shop. He's got his own restaurant and I saw Santa go past us in his sled with the reindeer and everything." Amber took a breath and then carried right on, "Santa's town, it's called North Pole, you know?" She shared knowledgably. "It's got lights and lots of Christmas trees and this huge toy store." Grabbing Bree by the hand, Amber didn't even notice the amused laughter of the adults. "Come see."

"Wow," Bree exclaimed, enchanted by her little one's glee. The toy certainly was impressive, taking up a huge portion of the living area. "It's really cool. You could play for ages with it."

"Uh-huh," Amber's head bobbed up and down vigorously. "Dad bought it for me. He said that it's my pre-Christmas present. I like Alaska, there's lots of presents here." Bree bent down and gave the miniature Santa Land the attention that Amber expected. It was a replica of Santa's house and the surrounding street and homes found in North Pole. Todd and Daniel had taken Amber there for the day so that Bree and Moira could finish the preparation for Christmas lunch the next day.

"It's really pretty, Amber." She kissed her daughter's cheek, happy to see the sparkle in her eyes. "Did you say thank you to your dad?"

"Uh-huh." Amber replied. The expression was becoming a favorite of hers. "Mom, you've got to say thank you too. You'll have to play with me, like you promised, because I don't have friends here yet, so you have to say thank you too."

"Of course," Bree turned to look at Todd who was watching the spectacle indulgently from his spot on the sofa. "Thank you, Todd. This is a lovely gift."

Amber cut off the response that Todd was about to give, "No mom! You have to say thank you properly. And, Daddy is family so you have to give him a hug and a kiss like I do."

Cursing the rule Amber and she had made up about how to say thanks to family, Bree made her way over to Todd with chagrin. If she refused to do so, it would indicate to Amber that Todd was not part of the family. "Thank you, Todd." She perched to give Todd a kiss on his cheek as he moved his face towards hers. In the living room, with their daughter keenly watching to see that they family rule was obeyed, their lips touched for the first time in seven years. It was such an innocent kiss, but it didn't explain the sudden heat she was feeling. Stunned, they both jumped apart after just a few seconds, although it felt like ages, they stared at each other with naked lust.

Amber's giggles broke through Bree's whirlwind thoughts and she quickly completed the ritual with a hug, avoiding frontal bodily contact as far as possible, making it swift and evading his eyes. To make light of the incident and to distract her from the pull of desire, she asked Amber, "Amber, honey, I think your dad will be playing with that too, so he should say thank you too, don't you think?"

Amber rolled her eyes and giggled, "Mom, don't be silly!" She exclaimed with such drama, making Bree and Todd giggle too and breaking the tension, "He can't hug and kiss himself."

"Clever girl," Todd praised. "I guess I'll just have to give you a hug and kiss instead."

Bree left the room while father and daughter, besotted with each other, exchanged hugs, kisses and smiles.

xxx

They were all in the kitchen, cleaning up after the feast that Bree and Moira had prepared. Todd enjoyed this Christmas more than any other in his memory. All the adults exerted extra effort to make Amber feel cherished and to give her a real family celebration. He lightly fingered the woolen neck-scarf, dominated by reindeers that his daughter had given him. It was the best Christmas gift he'd ever gotten. All he needed to top it off now was a kiss under the mistletoe with Bree, which she was determinately avoiding.

After stacking the last plate in the cupboard, Todd, the quintessential planner, pointed to his itinerary that was stuck against the fridge with Christmas-themed magnets. "So, what are we doing for New Year's? That's about the only gap on our schedule."

"On New Year's Eve, mom and I make popcorn and watch the countdown in Time Square. We have a disco in the lounge and I get to stay up late!" Amber suggested, "We can do that."

"We certainly could," Todd replied, "if you promise to save me a dance, young lady."

"I have a better idea," Moira announced. "I admit that I've been jealous of the time that you two," she waved a hand at Todd and Bree, "have been spending with my great-granddaughter. We'd like some time alone with her. So, how about you let Daniel and I spend some special New Year's Eve time with Amber and the two of you can have our tickets to the annual dance in town?"

Seeing the speculation in Bree's expression, she smoothly persisted, "Amber, honey, what do you say? Grandpa and I can sort through the attic with you and I'm sure we can find some costumes that will just need a bit of sprucing up. If I remember correctly, there's a disco ball up there too!"

"You're right Gran. I've been egglecting you." Amber's reply was so contrite that no one had the heart to correct her vocabulary.

"That's okay," Moira smiled at her sunshine girl. "You can make it up to us with our very own grandma, grandpa and Amber New Year's Eve dance and then your mom and dad can go out and have some fun on their own and not bother us. What do you say, honey?"

"I think that's a great idea." Daniel caught on to what Moira was doing; raising an eyebrow at her behind Bree's back, which she pointedly ignored. "I haven't been to a disco in decades." Daniel broke out into a dance resembling a chicken having a seizure that had them all hooting. Catching his breath at the end of his act, he looked at Bree and Todd. "Indulge us old folk, will you? Your Gran's also right in saying that you kids need to have some adult time and it would be good for the folk in town to see you two having fun together. Put to bed some of the nastier gossip that's probably going around."

Todd wanted to grin like he'd just hit the jackpot, but forced his expression to look thoughtful. "You're right. We could do with some good PR and a bit of fun in the mix, an opportunity to get to know each other again." He looked at Bree, quickly correcting, "It will help cement the good footing we've begun on as parents. Are you game, Bree?"

 She'd been cornered and could only acquiesce, albeit grudgingly. "Okay, if that's what works for everyone, I don't see the harm in it." Spending time in Todd's company, alone, wasn't going to assist her in battling the itch being with him was giving her. What's more, she didn't have anything to wear. Thankfully with the money she'd saved from Todd paying for Amber's school things and clothes, not to mention quite a few items for her, she could splurge on a dress and some heels. "I'll have to go buy a dress, though. Are there any new places in town that I can shop for something?"

Bingo, thought Moira. "Honey, I'm the wrong person to ask that type of thing. I have my few standards from way back. But, Shelly's still in town. You remember Shelly from high school, don't you?"

"She was my best friend through high school Gran," Bree offered a droll response. "I haven't forgotten her; I just haven't been in touch."

"Well she's the same sweet girl she always was," Moira countered. "In fact, she's opened up a swanky boutique to cater to both the tourists and the locals; you'll see that we have quite a few events here now. It's still new, but she's already quite busy so she must know what she's doing. Emma…you remember her?" At Bree's affirmative nod she carried on with the tale, "Well, she needed an urgent dress for some do for her son at the University. A cocktail thing. She found out about it last minute and gave Shelly's a try. She was quite impressed by what was in store. So, I'm sure Shelly will be able to help you out."

"Okay, it can't hurt. Amber and I can pop by the shop on Tuesday." Then she looked at Todd, thinking that she saw a self-satisfying smirk but it was replaced so quickly by nonchalance that she shook her head – she must have imagined it. It was probably her hormones going on over-drive being so close to him. It filled her with trepidation about a whole evening in his company without Amber to monopolize his attention.

Thinking quickly, Bree said, smacking her forehead forlornly, "I forgot, we're supposed to go snow-machining on Tuesday." She looked at Todd seeing an out. "And, your itinerary is still quite full for the rest week, so I guess we'll have to can it. I can't exactly go dressed in what I've got. Sorry Gran, Granddad, it was a sweet thought, but I guess it's a bit late notice to get a dress." It was hard not to look smug.

"Oh, that's not a problem at all." Todd wasn't going to let this little thing get in the way of the bigger plan. "I also haven't spent much time alone with Amber, so it can be our little adventure. I'll take her on the snow-machine and you can meet up with some of your old friends. Have some girl time." He didn't think she'd had much of that over the last six years. She obviously seemed so used to being around Amber twenty-four, seven.

Outmaneuvered, Bree nodded, feeling as though she'd just been played. "Thanks. It seems that it's worked out well then. I'll go to town on Tuesday and hook up with Shelly."

Chapter 4

Days filled were with continued sight-seeing, flight-seeing, and orientating Amber to Devil's Peak and the farm made the time to the dreaded New Year's Eve dance speed by. Bree focused her thoughts on Amber's face when she got to collect eggs from the chicken coop for the first time or her excitement when she went up in the plane alone with her daddy. Although Bree's heart had shot up to her larynx when her daughter flew above her, she'd been less anxious then than now, as she got ready to go to the dance with Todd.

Her palms were sweaty, face flushed, and eyes a bit brighter than normal. She had never been this grateful before for makeup – maybe someone would assume that her blushing cheeks was due to excitement rather than the unease that she actually felt. Bree gave herself a good once over in the full length mirror on her closet door. Her hair was loose and she'd kept her makeup to the bare essentials. Shelly had helped her choose a cerulean blue cocktail dress that ended just above the knee. Except for the color, the style of it was elegant in its simplicity, allowing her to wear the dress rather than the other way around. She wore no jewelry other than dangling diamante earrings that matched the only flashy thing on the dress, a lovely diamante adornment strategically positioned just before her waist to create the illusion of a completely flat tummy. The halter-neck satisfyingly emphasized the increase in cleavage courtesy of having carried and born a child. She carried matching silver and diamante strappy sandals and a silver clutch purse in her hands. Because it was Alaska and it was winter, she'd go in bunny boots and multiple layers of outer-garments, then change into her formal shoes and shed the extra layers when she got to the hotel. Alaskan women never let the weather stop them from looking good.

It reminded her of different times, different circumstances when she did just that in preparation for a date with Todd. Junior Prom, Valentines Dances, Spring Dances, and Senior Prom… what she'd give to have that back at that moment! Not at the expense of Amber of course. No matter what had happened, she was glad for her daughter - being a mom was the one thing she was most satisfied with. That and her studies.

Regardless of everything that had happened in her life, Bree allowed her to appreciate that she'd done well. Standing a bit taller, squaring her shoulders, and sucking in her tiny mummy tummy, she resolved to go with the flow that night. She was an adult. She'd been through worse, a lot worse. With that mantra complete, she headed downstairs to the living room where she heard Todd's occasional response to Amber's incessant chatter. Here goes…

Bree walked down the stairs to the picture of Amber, dressed in a multi-colored, glittery costume that represented disco to her six year old imagination. "Wow, mom, you look like a princess!" Amber's awestruck response was exactly what she needed to boost her confidence.

Bree bent down and kissed Amber, leaving the replica of her lips on her soft, rosy cheek. As she wiped it off with her fingers due to Amber's protests, she threw a glance at Todd. Sucking in a sharp, quick stream of oxygen, Bree pasted a smile and gave him a nod in greeting. She was unprepared for the undisguised lust she saw on his face.

Turning back to Amber she said, "Thank you for the compliment, Amber, that means a lot to me, coming from a real princess, of course."

"Oh, mom," Amber rolled her eyes at Bree. Another one of her little quirky mannerisms. "If I'm a princess and you're my mom then you're one too."

Lips curving, Bree responded, "Of course. I stand corrected."

"You look great! Beautiful!" Todd's simple remark laced with sincerity, made Amber giggle and her turn a bright shade of pink.

Todd was looking pretty good himself in a black pants and perfectly matching black shirt, casually opened at the top to reveal his delicious looking Adam's apple. Black only made his dark looks more devilish and broody, something women wanted to sink into. Unfortunately, with the way he looked, Bree felt like one of those women. He bent over to chat to Amber as she tugged on his sleeve in excitement. Bree sighed, it gave her a fantastic rear view that nudged the temperature up a few notches. Todd turned around and caught her staring at him. He grinned in response, which she duly ignored offering him a blank expression in exchange.

"Are you ready to go?" Todd asked, holding his arm out, ready for her to hook into.

Bree nodded, bending down to kiss Amber first and greet her grandparents. Not, yet ready to speak to this sinfully delicious version of Todd, she took his arm and left for town to the sound of giggles in the background.

xxx

"Bree Tanner Ramsay," a shrill voice interrupted her conversation with Shelly.

"Hi Sandra," Bree replied, keeping her voice light and interested. Sandra was one person she had not missed while gone from Devil's Peak. The feeling was as mutual as their common lust for Todd. From the looks, that Sandra had been throwing Todd the whole evening that seemed to be another irritating constant.

With a dress as brassy as her voice, Sandra dramatically stopped in front of Bree and gave her outfit an inspection. "I see that little has changed since you left us. I was hoping that some of the Lower 48 sophistication had rubbed off on you."

Bree discreetly nudged Shelly who was about to deliver a scathing retort and with a fake smile still pasted on, responded with the nonchalance, she was far from feeling. "Well, you know me Sandra; I'm just a hometown girl at heart." Before the verbal boxing match could be further entertained, Bree grabbed Shelly by the hand and headed over to the hotel bar, "Excuse us, hun, we're a bit parched. See yah around."

"Two things," stated Shelly, "first - you don't drink, and second - you're too nice to that cow."

"Killing her with kindness, Shelly," Bree laughed. Now, this was one person she definitely had missed. Shelly may be direct and come across as no-nonsense, but she was loyal to a fault.

"Uh-huh," came Shelly's skeptical response.

"Now what's the beef with Todd?" inquired Shelly. "You know I don't entertain rumors as far as the people I love are concerned, so you better tell me."

"Todd and I are trying to come to terms with co-parenting Amber," replied Bree.

Shelly quirked an eyebrow in response, "Honey, you can't fool anyone. Todd hasn't been able to take his eyes off of you the whole evening."

"That's just high school flames still burning, Shelly," returned Bree. "We didn't have closure when we broke up."

"As I recall," drawled Shelly, "you didn't break up. You upped off and left. And, from what I see, you still haven't 'broken up'." Shelly used a well-manicured hand to make air quotes before flipping her long, mahogany curls over her shoulder.

"And this is a good conversation. Thank you." At yet another quirked eyebrow, Bree laughed and carried on, "No, seriously. Maybe closure is what we need before we move on."

"Sorry to interrupt, ladies but I believe, Shelly that our dance is up." Shelly's date, a sinfully handsome newcomer to town, dragged Shelly away to the dance floor.

It gave Bree a moment to gather her thoughts. Closure. That was exactly what was needed. And, the sooner it was done, the better. She scanned the hotel bar cum dining area for Todd without any success. The evening had gone better than she'd imagined. They'd seemed to have put their differences aside and had even managed to dance together and have fun. They'd gotten quite a few looks when they'd arrived, but as the evening progressed, less people seemed focused on them, so the tactic to meet the grapevine head on must be working. What wasn't working was controlling the pull he had on her. It had seemed so easy, so natural to dance with him. Swaying in time to the music had allowed a number of intimate memories to creep in. Not cool and not what she needed right now.

"You're looking far too serious for a night out," Todd's voice interrupted her thoughts. He'd come up behind her and she could feel the heat coming off of him. Again, not cool. In fact, it was far too hot in the room.

Resisting the urge to fan her, she looked up into the chocolate warmth of his eyes and swallowed as discreetly as she could manage. "Oh, I'm just tired," Bree replied, shrugging her shoulders in nonchalance. "I haven't been out to a party in a while."

"Well, let's make it worth it then," the smile Todd threw as he held out his hand, lit the room.

"Okay," Bree squeaked, inwardly cursing.

The dance was the same torturous exercise in masochism as the previous ones. Their bodies moved in sync, touching teasingly when a dance move from either allowed a bump, a caress. The sudden cheers of, "Happy New Year," broke the spell woven by the dance and startled her, bringing her closer to him. And just like that, he leaned down, kissed her and it was as though seven years had not even passed.

The kiss was tender, sweet, filled with fondness, and banked heat. It was a mouth she was familiar with, a mouth she'd been craving without knowing. The touch of his hands as they slipped around her waist and drew her closer felt right as did her arms snaking around his shoulders to lightly tug him down, his hair was like silk between her fingers.

All too soon, the kiss ended and Bree looked up into eyes that had turned the brown of good, dark chocolate; kiss-swollen lips that had her wanting to close in for another nibble.

Taking a breath, she said, as steady as she could, "Happy New Year, Todd. I'm just going to freshen up before we leave," and she fled to the bathroom.

The drive back to the farm was awkwardly silent. When they arrived, Bree noticed that the only lights on in the house were on the porch and in the hallway. Thank goodness, she didn't need to fake a 'fun time had' to her grandparents.

Todd cleared his throat and turned to her with an expression that was hard to read. "I had a great time tonight. Thanks Bree."

Bree swallowed. It was easier to ignore the attraction in the quiet discomfort of the drive there. Face to face bedding down the internal sparks was a monumental task. "Pleasure…uh… thanks too," Bree squeaked. She took a moment, "I mean thanks. I had a great time too." Go figure that she'd act like a high school kid around her high school sweetheart. And oh yes, we was swooping in for the end of date kiss. Knowing his moves, Bree preempted it and scooted out the door before he could paste his delectable lips on hers.

Rubbing her arms to ward off the tingles of the cold and not in exaggeration, she blurted out, "Yikes, it's cold. I better get going before I catch my death. I actually forgot how cold it's here. See you tomorrow, Todd."

Later that night, Bree finally gave up on the succumbing to the dreamless sleep she so eagerly wished for and got up. Because she was alone in the privacy of her old room, she took down a box from the top of her closet. At the very top of the contents was a photo of her and Todd at the high school prom, a heart around their faces glowing with the love of hope, the love of teenagers, and in it was written "Todd and Bree forever." Sighing, she closed the lid and got back into bed, the heat she felt on the dance floor gone and her heart filled with aching loneliness and longing.

Chapter 5

Bree hurried into the farmhouse. It was hard to believe but the Alaskan cold had actually gotten colder. Not that the cold mattered much to Amber.

The previous day, she'd stood alongside her gran watching disapprovingly as her granddad and Amber had spent their time frolicking in the snow. Snowmen were built in as many varieties as they could be, snowball fights were held with her traitorous gran joining in and various skiing and sledding activities were engaged in. Her grandparents had been showing a huge burst of renewed energy and when she teased them about it, they attributed it to her return. Bree's lips curved at the lie - she was glad for the truth of the matter, which was that Amber had given them the gift of her unconditional love.

When Amber had skidded into the kitchen, dripping with snow and asking for hot coffee, Bree caved and joined them. The moment she saw Amber's awestruck face as they threw the hot coffee into the air and had watched it freeze, would be one that would stay with her for eternity.

Tires crunching on the snow alerted her to a visitor; it was too soon for Amber and her grandparents to be back from town. The wind had picked up, impacting visibility and she shielded her eyes, staring, until the blurry figure morphed into Todd. Despite her resolve to attempt a platonic co-parental relationship with him, she felt a clench in her gut. Despite the many layers of clothing, there was something about him that pulled at her - always had.

"Hi Todd," she called out from the porch and let him into the arctic entry. "What brings you around?"

Handing layers of clothing to Bree, Todd, shook himself as if that would chase some of the cold away. Darn, he knew a better remedy for cold and she was standing right there. Not that that would help much after the way she'd been acting as though he'd been invisible since the dance. If she weren't so skittish around him, he would've thought she was indifferent.

Soaking in the warmth of the house, he looked around searchingly, "There's a snowstorm coming, and I thought I'd pop by while I could to see Amber."

"Oh," Bree let slip. Darn it! Of course, he was here to see Amber. She'd known that. But then why on earth had she thought that he was there for her? "Of course," she quickly remedied. "Amber and my grandparents went to town for supplies. They should be back soon. Would you like to wait?"

The banging door of the artic entry made Bree jump and prevented Todd from responding as he went to close it. "Looks like the storm is here," he observed. "Are the men still working on the farm?"

"Nope," Bree responded. "They closed the hothouses with granddad yesterday and the chicken coop was seen to this morning so they're all gone."

Bree gnawed her lip, "Amber's never been in a snowstorm before. Let's call her."

"Bree, I'm glad you called," her grandmother's voice came through the static sounds of storm-whipped phone lines. "We've been trying to get through to you for ages."

"Sorry, Gran," Bree responded, "I got in a few moments ago and then Todd arrived. The storm's picked up here, so I must've missed your call, and the storm's interrupting calls coming through I suppose."

"Well," Moira stated, "the storms in full force here. I'm afraid, honey, that we won't be able to come back to the farm. The three of us will bunk with Mary. I'm glad Todd's there - means that he's stuck too and that you won't be alone."

Yep, thought Bree. Just great. "Can I speak to Amber please, Gran? If the lines get cut off, I won't hear from her for a while."

"Sure," Moira answered before putting Amber on the line.

"Mom," Amber began, "there's a snowstorm and the wind's howling."

"The wind's howling, honey," Bree smiled. Trust Amber to get excited about a scary snowstorm.

"Uh-huh," responded Amber. "And there's even more snow than before, but we can't go out because it's dangerous and Gran says that we have to stay warm and we can't come back because it's dangerous and we're staying in town and…"

Bree cut the verbal barrage off, a wider grin on her face, "And you need to be safe. So you know I won't see you until after the storm and the roads are cleared?"

"Yes, mom," Amber replied all-knowingly, "Gran told me."

"And you'll listen to Gran?" Bree asked.

She could feel the eye-roll Amber was giving as she replied affirmatively. "Now honey, I may not be able to speak to you again until I see you but I'll try, okay?"

"Okay, mom" responded Amber, "I love you."

"I love you too," Bree replied misty-eyed.

"Can I speak to my dad now?" Amber asked.

Bree handed the phone to Todd and puttered around in the kitchen trying, though not succeeding, to not eavesdrop. Regardless of their relationship, Todd had taken naturally to fatherhood and the bond he'd quickly formed with Amber was solid. That was what kept him in her life and made her make an effort around him though her body wanted to jump him and her heart wanted her to run away.

xxx

The wind screamed as it whipped around the house and scattered snow on every surface. While they still had television, they'd watched the news and the tales of people rescued from cars, animals brought into shelter was humbling. Bree was ever grateful that her loved ones were safe and warm inside homes built for this weather.

"What are you doing?" Todd interrupted her thoughts.

"I'm making hot chocolate," Bree answered. "All that snow out there makes me want something warm to drink."

Todd nodded in understanding, "The snows already a meter thicker than this afternoon and it'll get higher still. Let's hope this storm is a quick one as predicted."

"Yes," agreed Bree, "I've never been away from Amber before and I know she's okay, but I kinda just want her with me. I want to hold my baby."

Todd regarded Bree, a misty-eyed mom as she moved around the kitchen pulling cups out of the cupboard and mixing two cups. She didn't need to ask him - seems like she remembered that he had a fondness for the drink. He's eyebrows quirked when he saw her plunking a bottle of hard stuff on the counter. "Ah, Bree," he interrupted her. "You don't drink."

Bree looked at the bottle of fiery spirits in her hand and shrugged, "I do now."

"You're that worried about Amber?" he prodded. She was gnawing her lips again.

Yes, Bree, thought. I'm worried about Amber and I'm worried about being stuck in here with you. "Of course," she responded. Then shrugging again, she added a few tots to their hot chocolate, not noticing Todd's brows rise at her heavy hand.

"Bon appetite," she said, handing the piping hot mug of chocolate-laced spirits to Todd.

"Let's go sit by the fire. It's the best way to have hot chocolate," Todd suggested.

Sitting opposite Todd, a deck of cards on the table between them, she took a gulp of the liquid and choked, sputtering everywhere.

Todd pressed his lips to stop the grin from showing and went to gently smack her on the back. "Arms up," he said, "and breathe."

Freaking hell, holding her arms above her head with him behind her was not a good idea when it held so many possibilities - without clothing of course. He let his hands slowly glide down the insides of her arms and sides then nearly did a whoop when she gave up an involuntary shiver.

Bree cleared her throat and abruptly sat down facing the deck of cards and as far away from him as possible. "Should we play?" she inquired.

Todd nodded broodily, an observation that Bree forcibly ignored as she watched him reach out and cut the cards. After nearly an hour of terrible playing on both of their parts, Bree sat back and sighed in exasperation.

"That must be the worst game of cards either of us have ever played," she stated, sullenly.

Todd nodded in agreement. "I don't know about you, but I'm bored with playing cards. I remember us being much better at it - must be the storm and worrying about being away from Amber in her first snowstorm that's causing us to suck."

"Oh, I remember you always sucking," Bree responded.

"I remember differently," retorted Todd, "but I'll defer to the lady in this instance as our most recent match proves differently."

Todd sat back and sipped his now tepid chocolate drink. "Should we watch a movie instead?" Bree didn't respond and he could see the thoughts roll around in her head as she bit her lip in contemplation.

"I'll let you watch one of those chick flicks," he offered.

"You always hated those," she said.

"Nope, didn't hate them," he argued, "I watched enough of them with you when we were dating."

"That's because you wanted to get into my pants, Mr. Hunter," Bree retorted then immediately drew back from the conversation. That was so not the way to go in this conversation; not when they were stuck alone in the house with candles flickering everywhere.

"Darn it," said Bree in fake disappointment, "the power's out. It was a good idea anyway though."

"Oh, don't throw in the towel yet, Bree." He made for the staircase, "I'll make a plan. You just sift through the DVD's and choose something."

Bree took her time to flip through the DVD's, not seeing what kind of plan he could make, and wondering what the heck he was doing upstairs. Moments later, a proud Todd came into the room bearing a laptop.

"I left this with Amber the other night to play those girlie games on," he grinned at her. "It was plugged in so the battery should be able to give us a good few hours. You can choose two DVD's I reckon."

Drat! She watched Todd happily set up the Laptop on the card table and scoot it over to the sofa. To watch the tiny screen they'd have to sit right next to each other. Arguing with the seating arrangements would make a big deal out of it and might make him think that she had feelings for him. Feeling outmaneuvered, she stated, "I guess I'll go make us some popcorn. You still like butter on it?"

Todd looked up, meeting her eyes and nodded. Oh, boy. Maybe popcorn and something else, she thought, taking her hot chocolate with her.

When Bree returned, it was with popcorn, glasses, wine, and cans of soda. She'd left her mug in the kitchen, now empty of hot chocolate. She saw and blithely ignored his raised brows when he spotted the wine. Stuff it. She'd take courage tonight wherever she could get it, because her libido was wimping out on her.

"You didn't choose something," Todd said, picking up a DVD, "so I picked this one. I remember that you loved it."

Romeo and Juliet featuring Leonardo - just great! Exactly what she did not need - a movie about star-crossed lovers! "Great," Bree responded a bit too brightly. Her previously lingering fingers now decisively headed for the bottle of wine. Handing a glass to Todd, she took her own to her mouth for a big swallow. The stuff was as hideous as she remembered. She didn't have any philosophical objections to alcohol; she just didn't enjoy the taste. So, she just hadn't had any alcohol since her early experiments. Well, she was certainly making up for it tonight.

The movie was predictably sad and beautiful and with each lover's tryst, as uncomfortable as expected. During the movie, Todd had scooted closer and had even gotten a blanket out to cover them. It reminded her of how they used to do this as teenagers; only then, the excitement was a pleasurable one. Now, it was torturous.

Towards the end of the movie, Bree had forgotten all about her resolve to keep Todd away, her heart mellowed by the alcohol. Laying her head on his shoulder, she felt exactly as she had with him, in this situation, before. The feel of the warm wool covering his hard chest was comforting, his arm steady, and creating the cozy feeling of being held safely, lovingly. Inhibitions gone, she snuggled closer to him and snaked her arm around his waist, loving the feel of his hard abs against the soft wool. Wondering what it felt like beneath the wool, Bree slid a hand underneath and me with hot, searing flesh. The ripples fascinated her and she played along the ripples, giggling at the stirrings of desire that leapt within. She was beginning to really enjoy this movie-watching idea of his. Her hand hit the hard leather of his belt. Not liking it, she made her way to the buckle.

"Bree, I don't think that's a good idea," Todd's hand stopped hers from loosening the offending belt.

"I disagree, Todd," she answered, leaving her hand in his and slithering up to the side of his neck. Her tongue flicked over his warm skin. "Mm…" she groaned, "you taste good."

Todd was frozen. He really wanted to give into her and rid themselves of this lust they'd been carrying around and denying, but his sense of right wouldn't let him. He'd never taken a drunk woman to bed and he wasn't about to start with Bree. She deserved a lot better than that.

Todd grabbed both of her hands and held them to her side, careful not to hurt her. "Bree," he pleaded, "you're drunk, and I won't take advantage of you."

"Then let's just look at it as me taking advantage of you," Bree purred against his ear, her hot breath shooting shards of lust straight to his groin.

Todd got up, accidentally pushing her to the side. The laptop nearly got knocked off the table and he scrambled to steady it. Cursing, he straightened up then yelped when Bree stood right behind him, cupping his rear.

"Bree, stop it!" Todd moved to the other side of the room. Even drunk and not herself, she was beautiful, the light from the fire casting a golden hue around her. It was taking all his inner strength to not go to her and slate his need.

"I'm going to sleep upstairs and I'm locking the door," Todd stated. "We have a life together as parents and I'm not going to disrespect you with a one-night stand. I want you, Bree. I want you more than I can remember. And when we make love again, I want you fully aware of what we're doing because that's what you deserve."

"Fine!" Bree shouted. "Run away. Run away like you've run from everything in your life. Run away again from me. I'm used to it."

The last sight Todd had of Bree that night was of her sitting and pouting on the sofa, uttering a string of expletives and derogatory comments about her. They said that a drunken fool offered no lies.

So, the words she uttered banked the need, but the pain that replaced it, cut to the bone.

Chapter 6

Bree woke up with a pounding head. Groaning, she squinted around the room. The storm and natural twilight of the Alaskan day offered little light, but it was enough to hammer at her aching head. She'd slept on the sofa, her clothing, and the blanket bunched up. Embers'd turned to ashes in the fireplace and the laptop jogged her memory. She'd been watching a movie with Todd. The empty wine glass, a smudge of lipstick on it, hit home. She'd gotten drunk. She remembered that and she'd remembered … well… she actually didn't remember.

Smells were coming from the kitchen where Todd must be cooking up some breakfast. They were smells that made her want to hurl. Eggs had never done that to her before. Cursing, through the alcohol-induced fog, she realized that she was experiencing her first hangover. Frankly, she didn't see what the fuss was about. Bree lay back down and pulled the blanket over her head.

"Oh no, you don't," Todd stated, pulling the blanket down.

"Leave me alone, Todd," Bree croaked, her voice sounding like a frog, her throat parched.

"Aspirin and water," Todd held out a glass and a pill.

Nodding, Bree sat up slowly, the room whirling a bit at first. "Thank you," she said after gulping down first water, then pill, then water again. "Thank you," she repeated before lying down again.

"Nope," Todd stated, pulling the blanket completely off and grabbing her by the waist.

"What the heck?" Bree exclaimed as he threw her over his shoulder like a sack of potatoes and headed up the stairs. "Todd, put me down."

"I will soon, I promise," he stated, sounding too much like he was enjoying himself.

Todd unceremoniously plonked her in the shower and turned the tap on. "I would've undressed you, but I didn't feel like bearing scratch marks for the rest of the week. So, have the shower, get the fog out of your brain, and come get some breakfast. I've already put clothes out next to the bath."

Peeling off the wet clothes, Bree found a new target to aim her cursing at. As much as it pained her to admit it though, the Neanderthal did have a point about the shower. The pounding of the warm water on her skin, streaming through her hair had a way of washing away some of the haziness.

Dressed and feeling better, Bree joined Todd in the kitchen for breakfast. She didn't really feel like eating but under Todd's eagle-eyed stare, swallowed down little bites until again, he was right, and she started feeling more human.

"Looks like the predictions were right," Todd threw in, leaning back in his chair while she ate. He'd eaten the equivalent of a horse for breakfast and his stomach was still as flat as ever.

Oh! Stomach! Bree had brief visions of her hand trailing over his flat, hard stomach, teasing the little hairs along the path to his…Cripes! Was that real or a dream? There was no way to fool herself, it had been real all right.

"The storm is over, Bree," Todd interrupted her panicked thoughts and steamy memories.

"Huh?" Bree looked up at him, flinching at the concern showing in his eyes. "Oh yes, the storm. I'm glad it's over. I miss Amber." Taking their plates to the sink, she turned around and asked him, "What happened last night, Todd?"

"We had dinner, played cards, watched a movie, and you got a bit drunk," he replied.

"And that's all?" Bree quirked a brow in inquiry.

"Yep. Why? Did you have some steamy dreams about me, Bree?" Todd teased.

"No," Bree shook her head, "just asking as I've never been drunk before."

Todd threw her a lifeline and changed the topic, "Should we see if the phones are back up?"

"Oh, yes," agreed Bree, "I'd love to hear my," she stopped and looked at him; considered. "I'd love to hear our baby's voice."

xxx

"So, how are things with you and Todd?" asked Shelly, her voice and manner all business.

"Oh, I don't know," responded Bree. At the steely stare leveled at her, she continued quickly, laughing, "Don't look at me like that. I'm telling you truthfully. I don't know."

"He's been a bit odd lately," added Bree. "The day after the storm…"

"When you had a hangover," Shelly interjected, grinning broadly.

"Yes, you dog. And thanks for rubbing it in," Bree mockingly slapped her friend's arm.

"Oh, I remember a prim and proper miss who wouldn't let vile alcohol touch her lips," Shelly responded. "You bet I'm rubbing it in for as long as I can. About time you let loose a bit."

"Nuh-uh, ain't gonna happen," stated Bree. "That one experience was enough thank you."

"We'll see," was Shelly's cryptic response. "Anyway, you were talking about you and Todd."

"Yes," nodded Bree, "He's just been a bit distant since then. At first, I wondered if something had happened between us. I mean, I had all these steamy images from the night before, but he denies them."

"Steamy images?" asked Shelly, leaning forward expectantly. "Do pray, tell."

"There's nothing to tell," Bree grinned at her direct friend. "Did you not here the part about 'he denied it'?"

"Nope," Shelly shook her head disappointingly. "I was stuck at 'steamy images'. You gonna make those images a reality?"

"No," Bree stated, firmly.

"The lady doth protest too much," quipped Shelly.

"Oh, no," disagreed Bree. "This lady has been there, done that, and got the baby. And the only thing that lasted is the baby. Love like Todd and I had burns bright and fierce, but can hurt you if you're not careful. So, I'm not going there."

"Whatever works, Bree. You know I've always liked Todd and you deserve a good guy like that, but it's your life and I support you."

"Thanks hun," Bree gave Shelly a hug, oblivious of the gleam of mischief that touched her friend's face.

xxx

The next day, Bree decided to redirect her thoughts from Todd and explore the newer shops in town. Moving and settling Amber in had taken much of her time until now. With Amber at school, making friends and in a routine between grandparents and parents, she could take the afternoon off for 'me time'.

Despite the isolation of the town, it was picturesque. Pots may be empty of flowers and covered with snow but the buildings were freshly and brightly painted in hues of blue, yellow, green, and some sporting natural brick that complemented the trees and mountains surrounding them. Lights twinkled in the windows of shop owners who refused to take down their festive season décor and though the streets were empty, the shops had a steady stream of customers as people departed them and rushed to their cars. Seeking nurturance in the form of hot meals and drinks, the bar, and restaurants were stocked with happy customers.

Bree remembered her father's scathing remarks about the inadequacy of the town council. Although she believed that he would've still found fault despite the town being so well maintained, he'd have a lot less to criticize. He'd also found a lot to criticize with her. Stuff it, thought Bree, that's definitely not the thoughts to carry around with you when indulging in some retail therapy and thanks to the help in house and home from her grandparents and her new job, she could splurge a bit - even if her bags held more for Amber than her. She'd rarely had a spare penny to splurge on her baby. Shaking the maudlin reflections away, she dashed from the toy store to the neighboring grocer.

"Hi Paula," Bree greeted the woman who'd been a constant in the shop for as long as she recalled. She'd seen Paula age over the years, had been playpen mates with her children and now, she was shopping for school supplies for her own.

"Hiya Bree," Paula's face split into a huge, welcoming smile. "What brings you out in the cold?"

"Gran asked me to pick up the supplies she ordered," Bree responded. "I hear you had stock come in from Fairbanks."

"I did indeed, hun," Paula nodded, scratching around behind the counter for a piece of paper. "Got your gran's order. Now let's see… yes… this came in this morning. Okay, I just gotta round up the rest of the order."

"No rush, Paula," Bree made her way to the back of the shop where a small table and two matching chairs stood for just such moments or a bit of gossip catch-up.

"Oh, hun," Paula stopped Bree before she sat down, "won't you be a dear and grab that box next to the table?"

"Sure," Bree answered, setting the box on the counter by Paula.

"Thank you," Paula responded, "it's just been so busy today with the stock coming in and Jim being ill."

"I'm sorry he's still sick," Bree offered. "It's this horrible weather. Amber had quite a cold last week, too. Is there anything I can do?"

"Well hun, now that you mention it," Paula began, "I haven't had a chance to deliver that box. Would you be so kind and take it for me - it's just around the corner?"

"No problem, Paula, I'm happy to help and it'll give you a chance to get gran's order together too."

"You're a darling, Bree." Paula opened the box and double-checked the contents. "Yep, all there. And it's right next door."

"Next door? At Todd's?" asked Bree. Surely, he could've fetched the darn box himself.

"Yes, he wanted to fetch it himself. He's rather partial to that fancy coffee but he's alone as all the staff are off sick too and I told him not to worry. In this weather a soul needs a warm drink, you know?"

Grunting a polite reply, Bree took the box and went a few doors down to Todd's building. He was sitting in the same spot he had been when she first returned to Devil's Creek - again jotting down clients' telephonic requests.

Great, Bree thought, the dread lifting. She could drop the box on the desk, wave and dash back out. She'd go and grab a cup of coffee in the diner and give Paula thirty minutes or so to get the order ready. She'd just turned around when she heard the phone click and Todd greet her.

"Hi, Bree," his deep voice hit her like she'd never heard it before. "You were at Paula's?"

"Hi," Bree turned around, subconsciously smoothing her hair, she nodded, "and Paula asked me to drop that off, with you both being short-staffed today."

Whatever Todd's reply was about to be was cut off by the ringing phone, "Excuse me he said and picked up the phone," He'd just finished taking that call when another came through. Sitting down now, Bree noticed that he was looking strained, dark circles surrounding his eyes. His hair was mussed from him running his hands through them. Guilt tugged at her. He was after all supporting Amber in a style that was more than adequate and while she was frolicking about town, he'd been stuck here running himself out.

When the call ended, Todd took the phone off the hook. "Excuse me just another minute, Bree. I need to use the gents."

Eyebrows raised, she realized that the poor man hadn't even been able to do that. Check that, he hadn't probably eaten yet either. She needed no more encouragement; her baby would expect it of her as she should because she'd been raised that way.

Bree jotted a note down on the legal pad and dashed out the door. Moments later, she was back in Todd's building with bags of steaming hot food. "You look like you needed it," she said, breathless from rushing outside in the cold.

"You didn't have to do that," Todd said solemnly, touched by her care.

"You're my baby's daddy. Of course, I had to. Amber would rake me over the coals or kill me with verbal diarrhea if I didn't."

Ah, yes. Amber. Of course, that's why she was being kind. Heck, he was starving and he wasn't about to decline the piping hot meal she handed to him.

"Thank you," he said, before putting the takeout down to answer the ever-ringing phone.

"You're welcome," Bree responded. "Now scoot," she waved him away and sat herself down at the phone.

"What are you doing?" he asked. And why did he seem to always ask her that these days. The Bree of the past he'd known instinctively. This Bree was full of surprises.

"You go eat," she ordered, "and have a human moment. I'll take over the robot phone duty." At his raised brow, she bit out irritatingly, "I bore and raised a child by myself and got myself a qualification at the same time. I can most definitely answer the phone, take down orders, and not chase your customers away."

"Okay, okay," Todd held up his hands, "no arguments from me then. And, I didn't think that you couldn't do it. More like I don't think that you shouldn't have to do it."

"Been through this," Bree gave him an eye roll, reminding him of Amber. "Now scoot. I've got phone calls to take."

A few hours later, after many phone calls with the early Alaskan winter's night already settled over the town, Bree gladly accepted the steaming mug of coffee from Todd. She sat back and relished the taste of a good brew slithering down her throat. "Mm… that's good," she uttered in pure bliss. "I get now why you order it especially."

"Is it always this busy?" she inquired.

"We have our good days and our crazy days," replied Todd. "Today was one of the crazy ones. Supplies have been running a bit low with the storm and what Paula can't get for folk; we get for them, couriering from Fairbanks and other towns that have supplies."

"It's a good business," Todd continued, "we can only do the well-paying adventure tours in summer when the tourists throng here but in winter, this is our staple. And we provide a much needed service so that feels good too. An added benefit you could say."

"Thanks for helping out, Bree."

"My pleasure," she smiled back at him. "Now, I gotta get home. They must be worried."

"They're okay," reassured Todd. "I called them just before night hit. I remember how your granddad fretted when you drove to the farm in the dark. I reassured him that I'd follow you back. In fact, I'll spend some time with Amber and if it's okay with you, bunk there for the night."

"Uh, sure," Bree responded automatically, good manners having been ingrained into her DNA. "Amber will love that."

"I doubt we'll get any more calls as it is way after closing time." Todd got up to go around the office and began to prepare to call it a night. "Let me just grab my stuff and we can be off."

"Darn it," Bree said in exasperation. "I forgot about Gran's order from Paula."

"No hassles," Todd waved her concerns away. "I'll grab it tomorrow and bring it around after work. I'll be coming to see Amber anyway."

"Great," Bree smiled. "Thank you."

"No problem," Todd smiled back. "Now let's go."

Chapter 7

A few days later Bree found herself heading for the local hardware store. Her grandfather had begun preparing the soil in his hothouses to be ready for spring planting. It was still a while away but he swore that the soil needed to be nurtured and treated so that it could yield a better harvest. Not having much of a green thumb, she was happy to leave those details to him. Amber on the other hand, was looking forward to digging in the dirt and of course, having a license to look dirty went down pretty fine too. Fortunately, the local hardware store carried just about anything needed on a farm in small quantities and knowing her grandfather and his habits, they would've pre-ordered what he needed in time.

The musty smell of wood hit her first, then the sharp smell of paint and the unique iron-tinged smell of metal. Sitting behind the counter was Mrs. Stewart, a constant in the community that went back to when her grandparents were kids. Mrs. Stewart claimed that the pure, unpolluted Alaskan air contributed to her amazing ninety-odd years on the earth.

"Hi Mrs. Stewart," she called out, although she was right at the counter, Mrs. Stewart on the other side. The tiny woman sporting an unmoving cap of grey hair and hand-woven cardigan, sat knitting and grumbling to herself about winter bugs. "Mrs. Stewart," Bree repeated, louder.

Mrs. Stewart looked up with a start before her face split into a broad smile. "Bree, how nice to see you, dear."

After exchanging some pleasantries, Bree inquired, "Is Mr. Stewart around? I've come to pick up the hothouse supplies for my granddad."

"Oh, no dear," Mrs. Stewart answered, baffled. "I'm afraid that John's down with a bug. I sent him home when I called this morning and he was barking like a dog. He wouldn't hear of closing the shop so I said that I'd sit here. Everyone knows the shop and us so they can just get what they want when they come in. It took some arm-twisting, but he gave in. He didn't listen to me when he was sick as a boy and he doesn't listen as a grown man. But, you know what kids are like."

"I sure do, Mrs. Stewart. My Amber's the same. But, she just loves the outdoors here."

"Yes," nodded Mrs. Stewart, needles clicking between syllables. "The Alaskan air is the purest you'll find anywhere. It keeps you younger and living longer."

"Sure is," nodded Bree. Bree stood a moment, her head tilted in contemplation. "Would you happen to know where Mr. Stewart keeps the hothouse supplies?"

"Well as your granddad is one of the few that asks for it, I know it's not in the main part of the store," responded Mrs. Stewart. "Why don't you go look out back. It should be in the store room. That manure sure does stink, so it won't be kept in there." Mrs. Stewart pointed to the storage room leading off from the inside of the store.

"That sounds like a good idea," Bree nodded relieved to be getting the stuff. She didn't know who would sulk more - Amber or her granddad - if she didn't take their 'dirt' back to the farm.

The storage area was really an oversized shed located behind the store amongst many other bits of rubble and scrap material dotting the thinning snow in a haphazard manner; as though they'd been thrown there and forgotten. It wasn't a sight that melded with the crisp, clean feel of the snow nor was it a sight, she imagined, that the neighbors across from it cherished.

With a creek, the door gave way and she was met with the dank smell of stale air and pitch darkness. Fumbling around on the inside wall near the door, she finally located a light switch and flipped it. In contrast to the outside, the shed was neatly kept. Rows of shelves lined half of it holding various machine parts and larger tools. The other side showcased general farming material, which was where she'd probably find her granddad's 'dirt'. Determined, despite the heebie-jeebies the place gave her, she proceeded inwards. This place must be the perfect hide-out for bugs; warm, dark, and safe from the elements.

She heard a squeak, let out a screech, and jumped onto the nearest high surface, which unfortunately turned out to be a slippery bag of something. She lost her balance and landed on her side on the dirt-covered floor.

"Are you alright?" A familiar voice asked. Trust Todd to show when she least expected it.

"Ah, sure," Bree blushed with embarrassment. "I thought it was a nasty."

"Ah," Todd's face split into a grin, "still scared of bugs, huh? And you're still calling them 'nasties'."

Bree narrowed her eyes at him, "And you're still so smug about it." Bree thought she heard another scuttle and slowly, elegantly climbed up on the nearest, non-slippery surface.

Her response and climb was evidently hilarious to Todd because he broke into guffaws that had him gripping his stomach as tears streamed down his face.

"You're being a jackass, Todd." Bree's voice dripped with venom, her eyes narrowed on a guy that knew her too well under certain circumstances. When that just made him laugh harder, she cut through it in frustration, "Well for Pete's sake. Stop laughing like an idiot and help me look for granddad's dirt."

Well that got his attention she thought. Todd wiped his eyes and stood up straight, his lips curved broadly. "Sorry, honey," he apologized, "I needed a good laugh."

"Well I'm glad I could offer you your daily dose of comedy," Bree replied disdainfully. "Now will you help before I kill you?"

"I always liked it when you got all prissy with me, honey," Todd retorted. "It got the juices stirred up all good."

"Todd…" Bree warned.

"Okay, okay," Todd held up his hands as a sign of a truce. "What's your granddad's dirt look like."

Bree rattled off the names her granddad had given her and watched Todd scratch around and locate the bags of mature, plant food, and organic pesticides. When he'd stacked them all by the door of the shed, he went to her and held out his hand. "Coming?" he asked.

Watching him carry the goods, as corny as it seemed, had been quite a turn-on; there was something quintessentially hot about a man who quietly and confidently went about his business. Oh, I'd like to be coming, she thought, and then shook her head, mentally reproaching herself for her lapse in judgment.

She took his hand and felt somewhat safer walking towards the door. With relief, she reached for the doorknob and turned. Rattling it, she turned back to Todd, who was bent over the bags and about to heft them over his shoulders. Darn but if that sight didn't send tingles to her nether regions. And yet another sign, she mentally acknowledged, that she had to leave the shed.

Rattling the doorknob again, she spoke to Todd without risking another look. "Todd, I think the door's stuck."

"Can't be," he said, "Mr. Stewart may be getting on in years, but he'd never allow a stuck door situation."

"Huh," Bree looked at him puzzled. "Okay, regardless of Mr. Stewart's handyman principles and practices, this darn door is stuck. Come see for yourself," she indicated the door with a sweep of her hand and stepped away - but not too far into the shed.

Todd tried the doorknob and also did a fair bit of rattling. "It's not stuck," he said, "it's locked."

"Locked?" she questioned. "Why on earth would it be locked? It wasn't locked before."

"How would I know why it wasn't locked," he bit out irritatingly. "I just know that it's locked now."

"I can't stay in here, Todd," Bree felt panicked.

"Let's just call Mrs. Stewart and ask her to open for us," he offered.

"She's losing her hearing, Todd I doubt she'd hear us."

"I meant your phone. Call her on it."

"I don't have my phone," Amber stated. "I left it on the counter in my handbag. Use yours."

"I don't have mine either," Todd replied. "I came over quickly when Mrs. Stewart called to ask me to help you with the bags. Said that Mr. Stewart was at home sick and that she didn't feel right having you carry them all by yourself."

"Well aren't you just the knight in shining armor," Bree's sarcasm was thick. "So, Mr. Knight, get us out of here."

"I would if I could, Bree," he responded. "In fact, I probably could if you'd stop nagging long enough so I could think."

"Fine," she huffed, sitting on top of the bags of her granddad's dirt, closest to the door. "Think away, Einstein."

Steaming with irritation, she watched Todd under veiled lids as he went around the room, inspecting it for a way out.

"You won't believe this," he came towards her, "but there aren't any windows either."

"So, we're stuck here?"

"Looks like," he nodded, sitting next to her on a neighboring stack of bags.

"Todd," she said, worried, "it's not a good idea to be stuck during winter."

"I know, Bree. I'm hoping that the kids across the road will come by sometime or your granddad will realize we're missing and come find us."

Bree nodded bleakly. "Don't you think that Mrs. Stewart would remember?"

"Maybe," Todd replied, "but she's been losing her memory lately. too."

"The poor darling," Bree stated sincerely. "It must be hard to change in that way, especially after having been such a strong, vital woman."

Todd considered then shook his head. "Oh, I reckon that she's still as strong, as vital, just in a different way."

Bree's lips curved in appreciation for his sensitivity. "That's a sweet thing to say."

"I have my moments," Todd answered, looking down at her, his lips curved in response.

"Do you remember when we were stuck in the janitor's room at school?" Todd asked, trying to prod her mind away from her fears.

Bree smiled at the recollection. "Yes. The end of senior year - your hockey buddies decided that we needed a bit of privacy. That was quite a fascinating study of janitorial equipment."

Todd looked down at his crotch, "Is that what you call it?"

Bree laughed and nudged him in the ribs. "That was fun. They thought we'd come out fuming instead we'd looked like we'd a blast."

"Yep," Todd said, the smile dying, sincerity replacing it, "We always had a good time as long as we had each other."

"And we didn't inspect your equipment, as I recall," Bree reminded him. "We got to second base and then found the janitor's comic stash, his radio and all sorts of second home items. It looked like he lived in there whenever he could catch a break."

"I remember," Todd smiled. "That was the best time of my life until you brought Amber into it. Now, I'm having the best time of my life."

The surety in his voice as he made that statement brought tears to Bree's eyes. She found that she was relieved that he felt that way, touched that he, despite the way his daughter had come into his life, had put all possible nasty feelings aside, and focused on what was needed. In this case, it was pure fatherly love.

"Thank you for that, Todd," Bree looked at him through misty eyes. "It means a lot to me that you've grown so close."

"That's the easy part," he replied, "loving the way a parent should. Although I've missed most of her life thus far, I'm really glad you came home, Bree." A tear slid down her cheek and he gently wiped it away. "Thank you."

"Ditto, hun," she responded drawing a grin from him, one that spoke of people who shared instinctively. She'd loved the movie, Ghost, and had made him watch it over and over. The most romantic line in that movie had been "ditto," Patrick Swayze's response to "I love you" and they'd used it often with each other.

Feeling encouraged, Todd, took her chin in his hands, and tilted her face upwards, looking at it with a mix of familiarity and re-acquaintance. "I remember how beautiful you were." His voice was thick, husky, and prickled her insides. "You're more beautiful now," he said, before swooping down for a kiss. Like before, the kiss was tentative, slowly savoring instead of devouring. Like rediscovering a favorite childhood candy in adulthood and relishing in the taste, and texture.

Bree moaned and leaned into the kiss, her body twisting towards him, her hands first slack at her sides then snaking along to glide up his well-formed chest. She heard his sharp intake of oxygen when she tweaked his nipples, the way he liked it. Smiling against his mouth, lost in memories of the past, she moved around, not breaking the kiss, and straddled him. His body had filled out, muscled-up but it still felt the same, felt just right. Just as his hands did, alternating between kneading and cupping her bottom.

The kiss grew hotter, headier and they began devouring, replenishing their suppressed, mutual thirst. Todd's hands moved away from her bottom and inched up, discovering her warm flesh under the layers of clothing. Bree began moving against him, gently urged by his hands at the small of her back, giving into the kiss as desire overtook them both, sending them into that mindless abyss that only true lust can create.

The rattle of the doorknob jerked them apart. Panting and disheveled, they stared at each other, stupefied; reassessing if they'd woken up from a tantalizing dream of the past or an earth-shattering moment of intimacy in the now.

Mrs. Stewart's voice cut through their stupor. "Bree? Todd? Are you in there?"

Bree found her voice first, quickly adjusting her clothing, "Yes, Mrs. Stewart."

A head poked around the door and regarded them, "I can't believe I forgot to tell you not to close the door."

They looked at her in bafflement. Alaskans always closed building doors in winter. Not doing so was asking to freeze your behind off.

"With my son being sick, he hasn't had time to fix it," Mrs. Stewart explained. "He got stuck in here the other day and luckily I was waiting for a call from him and got worried. Joe next door came, checked it out, and found him. Else Lord knows what would've happened to my baby being stuck in here in the freezing cold."

Bree cast a glance at Todd and nodded in agreement. There was no need to upset the poor woman further with more questions. "That's okay, Mrs. Stewart," Bree consoled. "Your son got out okay and so did we, thanks to you. So all's well that ends well."

"Bree, why don't you go and make Mrs. Stewart a cup of tea?" Todd suggested. "I'll start carting the bags to the truck." And you can give me a moment to let the bulge in my pants go down before I advertise what we've been doing to the town, he thought.

Realizing what he was getting at, Bree's eyes flicked down to his crotch and widened. "Er…, okay," she stammered. "That's a good idea." Gently steering the older woman out the door, she stated, "Now, let's go and get you inside and settled and we can have a nice, cozy chat. I bet there are loads you can tell me about what I've missed the last few years."

"Oh, that would be wonderful," Mrs. Stewart said with such eagerness that Bree felt a twinge of guilt. Well, she'd make up for it by indulging Mrs. Stewart with an ear so she could natter on about seven years of saucy gossip.

Chuckling, Todd set to work on the sacks of hothouse supplies, feeling stirred up and glad to have something to put physical energy into. Hitting his home gym later would take some more of the edge off. The problem was that it just wasn't going to be enough.

Chapter 8

"So," Shelly leaned forward, elbows on the kitchen table and a mischievous gleam in her eye, "anymore steamy visions of our local hunk?"

Bree looked at her, a blush creeping up her neck and inflaming her cheeks. "That's so random, Shelly."

"Of course," Shelly acknowledged indifferently with a flick of her hand. "But, that's not the response I was looking for and your blush confirms your wicked thoughts."

Bree's cursed cheeks, blushed redder in response.

Cocking her head to the side, Shelly stared at Bree. "That's also not a normal response from you." Eyebrows lifting, she belted out, making Bree jump in her chair, "Uh-huh! You made the visions a reality! And it's about darn time too!"

"Shoosh," admonished Bree. "Don't advertise it to everyone."

"Who's everyone?" inquired Shelly, with skepticism. "Your gran is upstairs with Amber and your granddad and with them being sick, they're not likely to come walking in on this conversation."

"This isn't a conversation," countered Bree, "this is an interrogation. And speaking of our two patients, thank you for looking after them. Gran needed to see to the farm and I didn't like the idea of taking time off work when I'm so new."

"You're welcome," Shelly smiled. "And you're also changing the subject. But, I'll concede to you this time around. Next time, I want the details. I gotta head on home and call Laura to check. She's good at managing the boutique, but you know me, I'm a bit of a control freak, so I just need to make sure all went okay. Really, coming here did me a favor. Otherwise I would've fretted about leaving it in someone else's hands and probably would've gone into work."

Shaking her head, Bree grinned at her friend's true self-observation. "You're welcome."

After exchanging hugs, kisses, and seeing Shelly off. Bree headed back to the kitchen to finish up the chicken soup - a winter-bug curing remedy she firmly believed in. When she'd been beyond broke and Amber had gotten sick as a toddler, enough good, hearty homemade chicken soup helped speed Amber onto recovery and saved further medical bills and trips to the local clinic.

"Your toes look so cute, my baby," Bree said lovingly while spooning soup into Amber's mouth. Her baby looked so weak, but despite that and her tired eyes. Setting the soup aside, she leaned over and hugged Amber before commencing the feeding again.

Amber wiggled her sparkling toes, courtesy of a manicure given by an indulging Shelly. "I love them," Amber responded. "But, you mustn't call me 'baby', mom. We've had this conservation Mom. I'm a big girl now. Honey is okay or Amber."

"Conversation, big girl," Bree corrected both of them and received a brilliant smile from Amber.

"Granddad had this toes done too," Amber shared.

"Is that so?" Bree asked; a grin spread on her face while her gran softly chuckled. Her granddad was snoring away, his natural exuberance around Amber depleted by his mirroring cold.

"Uh-huh," Amber giggled. "I asked Shelly to and grandpa said something. Shelly told him not to be grouchy and he said okay. What's grouchy?"

Bree threw a glance at her gran who abdicated all assistance and then answered, "It's when you don't feel like you do every day. You feel tired and not all that well because you're sick."

"I feel grouchy too, mom," Amber said in a confessing tone.

Bree's heart hurt a little for her baby and she leaned in to kiss her. "I know, big girl. But if you eat, drink lots of water, and sleep, you'll be back to running around and playing in no time!"

"Is my little angel sick?" Todd asked, looking debonair in a formal pair of pants and shirt.

"Daddy," Amber's, face brightened at the sight of her dad, and held out her arms for a hug.

"Your mom told me you caught a cold," he said worriedly. "I didn't know it was this bad."

"Do I look bad, Daddy?" Amber asked disappointingly.

Todd caught Bree's eyebrow wiggles of warning and answered, "No, you look as pretty as a princess." The age-old compliment, used by Dad's to make their daughters feel better, worked and Amber beamed up at him. "I've got a surprise for you downstairs. I'm just going to go get it and I'm taking your mom with me to help, okay?" Amber nodded weakly in response, the excitement of a pedicure and manicure from Shelly as well as her dad's appearance having over-taxed her.

"Why didn't you tell me she was so sick?" Todd asked Bree when they reached the hallway.

The retort Bree was about to utter got stuck in her throat when she noticed his ashen face creased with concern, brows knitted. This was his first experience with Amber being sick, she realized and it tugged at her empathy. "Oh Todd, I know she looks really sick, but it's really just a cold. She'll be fine. She just needs some rest, the right food, and some medication. We're all, you included, giving her that and love and attention, so she'll be back to her chirpy self in a few days' time."

"You sure?" he probed, worry not lessened. "She's had a cold before?'

Bree resisted the urge to giggle. It was adorable that he was concerned, but he was having a bit of an over-reaction to the circumstance too! "Yes," she said gravely, lips twitching at the corners, which he thankfully didn't notice. "I'm sure. Look, I know as a parent you want to cuddle her and wish her better. And, because she's your child, she looks more fragile than she actually is. I promise."

Todd nodded, not entirely convinced, but looking more relieved. "Okay, let me take her the corsage."

"Oh, I forgot!" Bree exclaimed. "We all did. No wonder you're all dressed up. It's your daughter-dad dinner date. Amber was so looking forward to it too, but with her and granddad out for the count we all completely forgot."

Todd shrugged, "Really. It's okay. I'll take her out when she's better."

Bree smiled up at him gently. "You better go give our baby her first flowers."

The flowers thrilled Amber, a delightful traditional corsage consisting of baby's breath and tiny pink flowers. Flowers were not something that was naturally grown during the Alaskan winter so Todd must have paid a pretty penny for it, flying the tiny gift hundreds of miles, just to see a smile on his little girl's face.

"A pity about your dinner reservations," Moira quipped from a wing-back chair in the corner of the room. "Why don't the two of you go out, have some fun?"

"That's okay, Gran," Bree replied. "I appreciate your suggestion, but Todd and I couldn't enjoy ourselves knowing our big girl was sick."

"Oh, go on with you," Moira admonished. "Granddad's snoring and will most likely be doing that until the morning. And, Amber's just about to nod off herself. Her fever's broken and there's nothing more you can do, but sit and stare at her. You've been cooped up in this room or working and I think you need a break. And Todd," Moira threw a stern glance his way, "there's nothing you can do here either."

Amber, who'd been silently eavesdropping, piped in, "I want you to go to dinner, Mom."

Bree looked at Amber in surprise. Whenever she'd been ill in the past, Bree'd had to do much persuading to get her to stay with a sitter so Bree could go to work. That the sitter hadn't been a stranger, but their friendly neighbor and landlady, an elderly, kind-hearted lady with grandchildren of her own, hadn't made much of a difference. "That's a first, honey," Bree stated. "You've never wanted me to leave you when you were sick before."

"I know, Mom, but you never have fun and Daddy's the best fun. You've never eaten in a big person restaurant before."

Bree smiled and mussed her angel's hair. "That's because we had more fun at kiddie restaurants where you could play and got toys with your meals."

"Uh-huh," Amber nodded in understanding. "Those restaurants were way cooler. But, I'm okay. Gran's with me. She's going to read me a story from the new book Daddy bought me, while I drink milk, eat cookies, and then she's going to cuddle with me 'til I sleep."

Amber's face reflected eagerness for the treats offered in a way that only grandparents could. She hadn't left Amber alone with her grandparents for an extended period of time since the New Year's Eve dance. Softly touching her palm to Amber's forehead, it was met with soft, clammy skin that gave no indication that the fever was returning.

"Okay," Bree nodded, casting a glance in Todd's direction, shaking her head at his puzzlement to ward off further argument. Mercifully, a raised brow was the only challenge he gave. "But if I'm to go out, I better get dressed. Why don't you and your dad spend some time together while I get ready?"

"Yay!" Amber squeaked. "Gran, we're gonna have so much fun."

Grinning at Amber's enthusiasm and satisfied with her accurate evaluation of the situation, Bree went to her room. Only then did it strike her that she'd made her decision purely with Amber in mind, without recognizing that she was agreeing to a dinner at a possibly romantic restaurant with Todd. Yikes, she squealed inwardly. What the heck was she thinking?

xxx

On the way to the restaurant Todd received an education in childhood illness. That was thankfully something that he had no experienced with. When he and his siblings were very young, his mother had not been in a self-pitying, drunken stupor most of the time, so she had been able to still care for them at that point. The more Bree enlightened him, telling him Amber's whole medical history as well as her various reactions to being sick, the less anxious he felt.

Unfortunately, it also meant that he became more aware of Bree and the challenges he faced in getting them back together again - at least in bed and on paper. She was right when she said that they'd bonded well and speedily and he was anxious to have Amber with him fulltime in his home with both of her parents present. A phenomenon he'd longed for, but had barely been privileged to. Mentally brooding whilst keeping up with the light-hearted chatter Bree was maintaining, he continued to ignore the 'elephant in the room' as he led her into the restaurant.

The Lodge was one of the newer establishments in Devil's Peak, catering to tourists who wanted to experience Alaska at more of a distance than the older establishments offered.

"This is beautiful," Bree whispered, awestruck. The lobby of the hotel was elegant in tones of cream and champagne, a theme that was carried through to the restaurant. "It must have caused quite a stir with the locals."

As are you Todd, thought nodding, unable to take his eyes off her when she shed her coat and scarf. She wore a flowing back dress that left her long, elegantly-shaped arms bare. It was just to the knee so her great legs were free to his eyes and while not revealing, it was darn provocative. It nipped in under her substantially larger breasts and tempted a man to snake his hands up the floating skirt and hike it up. Lust hit hard and strong. He really needed to get her into his bed and soon.

Bree stared at him, waiting for a response. "Sure did cause a stir," Todd nodded. "But the town council handled all the changes well, positioning The Lodge as just another required one. The owner's local too - that helped." At Bree's frown he explained, "You remember Jack Thornton?"

"Jack? The sophomore that irritated the crap out of me, our senior year?" Bree asked, flabbergasted.

Todd grinned. "The one and same. But he's okay really. He only irritated you because he had a crush on you."

"But he can't be above twenty-four. How'd he do this?"

"Drive," replied Todd. "He went to the Lower 48 after high school, developed some computer program, made millions and came back a success. I know he irritated you and frankly, if someone moped around behind me with every step I took, I'd feel the same. But, you ladies didn't always see what happened in the boys' locker rooms. He wasn't physically bullied, but they sure did pick on him. I tried to intervene when I caught it happening, but I wasn't exactly round the guy twenty-four, seven."

"Well good for him," Bree responded.

Todd smiled. "I know what you mean. It's always great to see folk, you know, do well."

He held out his arm for her to take as the host showed them to their table. It was a beautiful setting. Very French - or what she'd seen French looked like in the movies - small tables comfortably seating two or four were scattered around the dining area, covered by long, ivory tablecloths that complimented the warm wood of the bistro-styled chairs. The soft notes of a piano, gently caressed by masterful fingers, emphasized the ambiance, and relaxed the diners. The far side of the restaurant was comprised entirely of floor to ceiling, ivory-painted French doors that led out to an expansive lawn and even wider lake. Their table was situated in front of the doors. Two chairs opposite each other, with a third holding an oversized stuffed toy, in front of it, a prettily-wrapped pink box that looked more like confection than a gift.

"This is adorable, Todd," Bree smiled up at him when she was seated. She leaned over and touched the soft, silky fluff of the polar bear ballerina decked in a pink puffy tutu and matching tiara. "And what is this?" She indicated the box.

"A man does not tell on one girl to another," Todd responded, with mock firmness.

Picking up the box, Bree shook it, heard rattling. Shaking her head, she looked up at him. "You know I hate not knowing things. So spill. I'm her mother."

"That ploy won't work with me, honey," Todd replied, smoothly. "Put the box down and stop staring at it. Amber can show you once she's opened it."

"You're no fun," Bree replied, pouting.

"And you're like the little girl who can't wait for Christmas," he laughed.

"Oh, well," Bree shrugged. "I'll see soon enough."

Todd signaled for the waiter. "Please, won't you put the gifts in my car?" he asked.

"Certainly sir," the waiter replied stoically, garbed in an equally sever looking black suit and starched white shirt. He efficiently and noiselessly removed the gifts and walked towards the restaurant exit looking odd carrying a large stuffed toy and equally girlish gift.

"This definitely isn't the Devil's Peak norm," Bree stated, gaping after the waiter. "If this was any of the places in town, we would've had the waiter sitting down with us and having honed the craft of needling information out of people, you would've spilled on what was inside that box."

"Come to think of it," Bree continued, "let's go to one of them."

"Really?" Todd asked. "All the local women love coming here on dates."

"Is that so?" Bree quirked a brow in question. "Have you brought any local ladies here?"

Cursing his slip, he scowled, "A few."

Bree laughed, "That's okay. I was just teasing you. I didn't expect you to have lived like a monk these past seven years, Todd." The words felt right, but in reality, jealousy had snuck in, Bree acknowledged. Which was ridiculous, because they weren't an item.

"So, have you seen other people?" Todd ventured.

"One or two," Bree responded, "but nothing serious. Being a single mom doesn't lend itself to wild romances."

Todd leaned back, unable to keep a satisfying smirk from showing. "I remember our romance as pretty wild."

"Yes, it was," Bree smiled back. And look where it got us.

"Bree, Todd - welcome," a strange masculine voice interrupted and saved Bree from further questions about her love life. "It's great seeing you again."

Bree looked up at one of the hottest guys she'd seen in a while. He was suave, oozing sophistication and dashingly debonair in an expensive silk suit of grey, a midnight black shirt under it. The guy had it going on - green eyes, dark brown hair, and a face chiseled by a master.

"I'm sorry," Bree said to the stranger. "I haven't been back in a while, and so much has changed. How do we know each other again?"

"Much may have changed here," his smiled at her, dazzling with teeth so straight they must've been cosmetically attended to, "but you're still as beautiful as I remember, if not more so."

The line was so much like the one Todd had delivered in the hardware store's shed, Bree darted a glance at him. Todd had his poker face on - not a good sign.

"Bree, this is Jack, one of the town's new businessmen," Todd interrupted the flirtatious glances; he'd had enough of them. "We knew him in high school."

"Oh yes, Jack," Bree responded, throwing a smile at him. "You've grown up since I last saw you."

Jack's smile slipped and Todd chuckled softly. "Yes, well," Jack responded, "seven years will do that to a person. Thank you for coming to The Lodge. I'll leave you to enjoy your dinner, but if there's anything you need, just let us know. Bree, lovely to see you again; we should do brunch sometime - The Lodge is renowned for it." He looked at Todd, nodded by way of greeting, and smoothly glided away from them to the other tables.

"Brunch?" asked Bree. "Is he for real? The only people that 'do brunch' are those who don't live on a farm in Alaska with a six year old kid."

Todd chuckled, "I guess he still irritates you." Something he was immensely relieved about. "You sure know how to take a man down, Bree."

"Oh, he doesn't irritate me," Bree stated artlessly. "He's just changed that's all and that caught me off guard."

"I noticed," Todd replied. "Like what you saw?"

"Well, he's certainly grown up. He's not the stick thin boy from high school. Why?" she asked. "Are you jealous?"

"Of course," replied Todd, searing her with a possessive look. "I'm here with you."

Bree gulped, dismissing the tingles that his look evoked - time to change the subject. "So tell me about this brunch business? I've seen the improvements to town, but what else do I need to know about?"

In the end, they had a relaxed dinner discussing old friends and new. Bree told him of her landlady and the people she'd worked with in Columbus. Todd told her about starting up the business and the many people he'd met. They avoided talking about each other, but for once, they didn't focus their entire discussion around Amber either. Todd paid the bill, tipped the starched-up waiter heavily, and helped Bree to the car thinking that the evening had turned out to be a success.

Chapter 9

Bree slid her key into the door of the farmhouse, Todd behind her carrying Amber's gifts. She turned the doorknob and was met with resistance. What was it with her and doors lately! "Todd, the door's stuck," she whispered. The house was in darkness and she neither wanted to wake her tired gran nor the two patients. "I've turned the key but it won't budge."

"Here, let me try." He handed her the gifts and took the key from her. "The latch is up. You're not going to get into the house this way unless we break down the door."

"Poor Gran," Bree stated sympathetically. "She's been covering for granddad a lot with the farming. She must've been so tired she didn't realize what she was doing. Maybe there's a window or something open. You could boost me up."

They went around the outside of the house, inspecting the building for any opening that presented a way in. "There's nothing. They're locked tight. Maybe the guest cottage is open," Bree offered.

"Hasn't that place been closed for a while?" Todd asked. "You guys haven't had any guests stay over in some time."

"I've wondered about that," Bree stated.

"I guess they've wanted to keep you guys to themselves for a while and their friends have good hearts but are nosy," Todd offered.

"Could be," Bree acknowledged. "Amber was playing there the other day. She treats the place like one big dollhouse, so maybe it's open."

After meeting with another locked door, Bree turned to Todd. "I didn't want to wake gran, but I guess I'll have to."

"You do have an alternative," Todd stopped her fingers from punching the farm house's number into her mobile.

"What?" Bree asked.

"You could stay at my place and I'll run you home tomorrow night."

Bree had not thought of that at all and it was not an alternative she was okay with. "That's sweet of you, Todd, but with Amber being sick, I'd rather be close-by."

He dipped his head in understanding, "Then dial away."

"She's not picking up," Bree said minutes later. "She must be exhausted. What if Amber calls for her and she doesn't hear?"

Noting her concern, Todd took her hand and squeezed. "Your grandmother raised you and your dad. She's got looking after sick kids covered. Besides, I've heard that moms have an inner-alarm built in that alerts them to when their kids need them. That should apply to grandmothers too."

"You're right," Bree acquiesced. "I'm being paranoid. Seeing how I doubt granddad would appreciate us breaking down the original farmhouse door, is the offer to bunk at your place still available?"

"With pleasure," he responded. "And don't worry about Amber," he gave her hand another squeeze, "you can call her first thing in the morning and I'll bring you back after breakfast."

"Thanks," Bree agreed. With her concerns about Amber placated. She realized that she'd be stuck under the same roof as Todd for the rest of the night. Heart-rate speeding up at the battle ahead to resist the tempting prospects it offered, she got into the car with an odd mix of trepidation and unwanted excitement.

xxx

Todd let Bree into his house, switching on the lights as they moved through it to the living room. He shot a glance her way, assessing her face. She hadn't said much since they left the farm. "Can I get you something to drink?"

"No, thanks," she replied. "I'm okay for now."

"If you change your mind, the kitchen's down the hallway at the other end of the house. I should probably show you around and get you something to sleep in."

"Thanks," Bree repeated and followed him. They'd never spent the night together - the whole night - when they dated before. Being alone with him in his home felt odd, intimate.

When she'd been here previously, it was to pick Amber up from a play date. Amber had a few friends from school nearby and Todd was always eager to show her off. Being that it was important for Amber to form bonds with other children in her new town, Bree had agreed to the arrangement. So, she'd only ever seen the front end of the house, not daring to step into his parlor so to speak.

Now, as she followed Todd through the house, she hadn't just stepped into the parlor, she was way inside of it and in danger of allowing herself to be devoured. She could feel the sexual tension between them, hovering in the air like an unspoken secret that everyone knew about.

Bree shifted her focus away from his well-carved behind to their surroundings. While she'd been ogling him, they'd moved down the hallway, past a dining room, home office and into a vast kitchen.

"Ooh," Bree purred gleefully, stepping into a cook's dream. The kitchen was large and airy. Huge windows would allow light to stream into the room during the extended summer daylight. It was fitted with every modern appliance you could think of and ample cupboards hinted that it held even more cooking wonders. "I don't recall you being very fond of cooking."

"When I got back after my dad died, my mom was even more internally focused," he shrugged. "So I had to learn to cook. I figured out, that I wasn't half bad at it and kinda enjoyed it. So, now I put out the odd dish or two."

"Well this looks a lot more serious than the odd dish. This is practically half the size of the bottom part of the house. Was it like this when you bought the place or did you do some renovation work?"

"Nah," he answered, "the kitchen was tiny - like the type you find on a ship or train. I figured that since I had to do it over, I might as well do it right. Build for the future." Now, that he said that, he could picture the three of them having a family meal at the table to the one side of the room. It was modern, but still cozy. He was a guy after all. Bree and Amber would add their own touches, soften it a bit. "You guys should all come over one Sunday for a meal. I'll do a pot roast and the works."

"I'm impressed," Bree said. "You said that Jack had done well earlier. To my mind, you've done pretty well yourself."

"Thanks," Todd replied, looking embarrassed. "You've done well too." At her cynical look, he explained, "No really. You've managed to acquire a professional qualification, a job in that profession in a place that does not have an abundance of employment available and you've raised a beautiful girl; our daughter. I don't think I've thanked you for that. So, thank you, Bree. I couldn't be a prouder father and you're largely to be congratulated for that."

Enchanted by his sincerity, embarrassed by his thanks, she made a study of the nearby counter's contents and mumbled a thank you. "I'm still ashamed of how long I took to tell you. I'm sorry for that, Todd. It's something I'll never forgive myself for."

Todd walked towards her and took both her hands in his; heightening their physical awareness. "You're both here now. That's what counts," he replied and leaned down to kiss her. The sexual tension they'd been carrying around exploded into an all-out lust seeking satiation. The kiss wasn't gentle, it was all-consuming, powerful, and lips took, bruised, bit, and sucked. Filling in as much as possible and drinking in the passion offered. Drinking in her kiss, Todd backed Bree up against the kitchen wall, hands flanking but not touching her.

The icy wall jolted Bree out of the passionate fog. Gently, she put her hands against his chest, fighting the urge to rip at the material and touch that firm, hot piece of flesh, and pushed him away.

Todd looked down at her and asked, "What's wrong?"

"Nothing," Bree stated in a voice laced with regret. "I just need a moment. Don't get me wrong. That was unbelievable, better than I remembered, but it's a bit soon. We're moving too fast for me and I need some time, Todd."

"You've been here for months, Bree." Todd pointed out.

"Yes, but our relationship was on tentative ground then. It took a while to get into a rhythm as co-parents, and then to get along again. Now this, this has been fast, and hot. I need to cool down and think."

Todd nodded; his head understood but the hardness in his crotch was yelling at him. "Okay, we'll take things slow." He leaned down and kissed her again, gently, sweetly, and with a subtle feel of yearning. "That okay?" he asked sincerely.

Bree nodded and to show that she was, she leaned up and delivered a kiss just as soft, just as sweet. "Now, show me the place upstairs Mr. Hunter."

Todd held out his arm to indicate that she should go first and had his turn at ogling her rear as it sashayed up the stairs. He grinned wickedly; he hoped she could feel his eyes on her the way he'd felt hers searing his butt earlier. It would serve her right after the 'go slow' request. Darn, but he understood what she meant. He just didn't like carrying around his lust like a ball and chain - it was damn uncomfortable.

The upstairs comprised of two bathrooms and three bedrooms with the main bedroom boasting a balcony with a view of the surrounding mountains and evergreen trees. Bree stepped out into the icy cold night and looked up at nature's fireworks, the Northern Lights. "That's one thing I missed," she pointed upwards. "There's nothing else like it that can fill you with so much awe, give you such hope because of its beauty yet make you feel so insignificant."

Todd thought back to the first night of her return and the similar thoughts he'd had. Taking her chin in his, he leaned down for another short kiss. "Let's go inside, we're not dressed for the cold out here."

"Let me look for a toothbrush. I should have some in the bathroom cupboard. You okay with sleeping in a t-shirt?"

"That will work," Bree replied.

Todd waved his arm towards the closet, "Help yourself."

Bree opened the doors, pulled out the drawers, and located his t-shirts. Sifting through them, she found his high school hockey captain's shirt. With a smile, she picked it up and smelled. It smelled like fabric softener, but she could vividly remember the spicy scent of excitement that had leapt from it when she'd leaned into him after he'd won a game. Putting it back, she pulled out another and shut the drawer. Sifting through his clothes felt intimate, personal as new discoveries melded with fond memories.

Jeesh, what the hell was wrong with her? She sat down on the edge of the bed. Todd entered the room a toothbrush in one hand, clean towel in the other. He spotted her and smiled and just then, she knew what was wrong and what she had to do. "Did you find a…"

Todd's question was cut off as she made the leap and clamped her lips on his, pulling his head down towards hers. Hard, debauched, ravenous. Fire erupted searing skin, burning through the doubts of the present, and the pain of the past. Fire consumed, stoking their passion, and flowing around them.

"I need you," Bree said, from shy girl to vixen, she stood before him, and then pushed him back onto the bed.

Todd was speechless. A myriad of thoughts raced through his mind at once, confusing the hell out of him. Desire flamed and he didn't give a damn. All he could see was the woman that he'd been lusting after for longer than was right for a healthy man. He had struggled to make peace that she wasn't his anymore. Now she was standing before him with the singular mission of rocking his world. And darn it, but he'd take that and give it back. He had no intention of leaving her any other way but limp, drained, completely, and hedonistically sated.

Bree's carnal intentions left no room for thinking. As soon as he'd thought that, she was stripping out of her clothes. Skin - loads of glorious skin, golden and tempting, just waited for his tongue, teeth, and lips. And, even that wasn't enough. He wanted her so bad, he wished he could crawl into her skin and devour her.

Bree took her time to undress, first slipping off her shoes, cheekily tossing them to the side. Toes had never looked that delectable to him before. Letting his gaze run up from her feet to her calves, and then slowly waiting in anticipation as inch by inch, she teased the dress off and chased away the dark covering. The dress, when pulled up, revealed lace and silk. More teasing as her beautiful, bountiful breasts continued to hide behind a scrap of lingerie.

Todd swore he was as hard as concrete, and obsessed with the need to cover and claim her.

"You leave me mindless," Todd rasped. "You're what every man wishes they had and what I'm privileged enough to experience."

Getting up from the bed, he kept his eyes on hers, making his intentions clear. They spoke of indulgence at the most basic, most pleasurable level. They spoke of an inferno of carnal passion. Like a predator stalking its prey, he moved towards her then not touching, let his gaze run down every inch of her delectable curves, touching her golden skin with his eyes. He allowed his gaze to move on, linger at whim, caring only for letting them feast on what he'd so long been denied.

Bree felt it, felt his hunger tease her, taunt her, and play with her. He stared at her neck and she shivered, moved his gaze to her breasts and she arched wanting more, only to have those wicked chocolate browns move swiftly away to give lighter caresses somewhere else. Moaning, she ran her hands over her body, following the trail left by his lascivious observations. The fire continued to consume them until they became the flames sprouting forth from it, flicking, playing, and dancing with each other.

Finally, after he'd returned the favor by slowly stripping his clothes off as he walked around her, he moved so that her back pressed into him. Bree felt the evidence of his desire. Rock hard against her flesh. Moaning, fantasies of it entering her, filling her drove her wild. She tried to turn and pull him down to her, but he held her fast, steady so she had no choice but to continue being subjected to his erotic torture.

"I need you, Todd. Now," she ordered.

"No," was all he said in response. Moving in closer, he allowed their flesh to meet so that her back was flush with his front. Grabbing her chin, he tilted her head sideways and leaned down, purposefully, slowly, not allowing their locked, heavy stares to break. Lips met, tongues danced and the flames continued to flicker and burn, searing until only flesh was left, only flesh mattered.

Bree purred, wiggling against him, returning the torture wantonly. She was a wet flame; sensuality personified and had never felt so damn sexy, so desirable before. The more they kissed, the more the sensations grew, the brighter the flame burned. Todd started caressing her and she felt alive, her skin prickling to attention under his hands. No longer flickering, the flame roared as he touched every part of her body that his long, strong arms could take into his masterful hands.

"Need it now," she growled.

"No," he repeated. Then he led her to the bed, allowing her to turn. Bree whimpered in relief, expecting him to fill her only to arch up from the bed as he trailed his mouth over her body, letting his tongue flick, suck, and taste. Bree didn't think she could burn hotter, but she did as he stoked her desire until the flames burst and she cried out in pleasure.

After her release, with him still leaning above her, she wiggled, breathless, but still unsatisfied. "I need…" she began then screamed out in pleasure when he plunged into her. Finally joined, the flame burned to new heights taking them with it.

Chapter 10

They lay together in the aftermath, flat on their backs in the bed - chests heaved in search of oxygen, and bodies were paralyzed after their erotic exertion. The bedding lay strewn over the bed and tangled with clothing on the floor. The air was tinged with the spicy smell of sex.

Breathless and dripping, Todd glanced at her and asked, "What was that?"

Smiling wickedly, Bree teased, "Oh, I think you have a pretty good idea of what we just did."

Enchanted by this confident vixen, he grinned, "Yes, I do and no, I don't." At her perplexed expression, he laughed and kissed her forehead. "No way can you frown after that."

"I mean," he explained, "what changed your mind?"

"Your hockey shirt," she stated simply.

"My hockey shirt? The one from high school?" He heaved himself from the bed and made his way to the closet. Determinedly opening the drawer and locating his hockey shirt, he pulled it out. "This?"

"Mm…" she purred in agreement. "It's such a turn-on."

Shaking his head, he grinned and joined her in bed, swooping her into his arms so that they lay comfortably exhausted. "I'm never getting rid of that thing. I'm putting it into my arsenal."

"You do that," she chuckled.

"Seriously, though," he prompted, "what changed your mind? Not that I'm complaining but one minute I was preparing myself to try to sleep with yet another hard on and thoughts of you and the next you became my hottest fantasy turned into reality."

Bree turned around so that she faced him, "I honestly can't say. It just felt right, like it was time. We've been circling around our attraction to each other since I came back to Devil's Peak and it seemed nonsensical suddenly. I'm glad I jumped you though." Bree grinned at him, trailing her fingers across his chest, loving the feel of this Todd, with ripped, masculine muscles, and the more mature physique than that of the high school boy she'd known.

"Believe me, I'm gladder than you are," he smirked, satisfyingly.

Bree smiled up at him and a yawn slipped through. "This is comfy," she said, turning around so that she lay spooned in his arms. He kissed her head with curved lips and snuggled into her. Within moments, they fell asleep, one hurdle of their romance crossed.

xxx

Bree awakened from a dreamless sleep, to the feel of a heavy arm trapping her. Looking at the clock next to the bed, she saw that it was still the early hours of the morning. Strange - she must've gotten in about two hours of sleep but felt as though she'd had a full night. She tried to stretch, but her legs were trapped, entwined in his larger, heavier ones.

"What are you doing?" Todd asked, looking at her with heavy-lidded eyes.

"I feel a bit stiff so I was trying to stretch," she replied.

"I have a better remedy for that," Todd stated, solemnly.

"You do?" she coyly inquired.

"Oh yes," he moved in and kissed her then got up from the bed.

"Where are you going?" she called out as he went into the bathroom.

"Just wait and see," he hollered back.

"Todd, you know I hate surprises. I'm too nosy to wait for them."

"Sure I know, but you know I like giving them and you'll like this.
Trust me."

The sound of running water and the spicy scent of bath oil filtered
through from the bathroom. "Not that much of a surprise, but
appreciated nonetheless. I could do with a bath. Thank you."

"Oh, this bath will be a surprise," he grinned at her with the devil in
his eyes. Oh boy, she thought.

                                    xxx

"I feel like putty," Bree said. "My body feels thoroughly used."

"Ditto," Todd grinned back. He was grinning so much that his
cheeks were starting to ache.

"That was amazing. I don't think I'll ever see a bath or full body
massage in quite the same light again. "You've corrupted me."

"I don't know about that," challenged Todd, "what you can do with a
towel astonishes me."

He let his fingers trail along her body, the gentle caress of loving and tenderness, not lust. His hands came to tiny bump between her waste and he splayed his fingers across it, wondering at the miracle she'd carried within for months that had turned into such a vivacious, precious girl.

Bree gently moved his hand away. "Why do you keep doing that?" he questioned. "Whenever I touch your stomach, you move my hand away."

She grimaced, "It's my 'mummy tummy'." At his confused silence, she explained, "It's a bump, i.e. it's not flat and sexy. It's flabby."

Todd sat up and like a typical guy, had a closer look. "What flab?" He asked, prodding at her stomach with concentration. "There's nothing flabby about it."

"You're being nice and that's sweet," Bree turned around onto her stomach to look at him and hide the offending part of her body away from his curiosity. "I've had a child and most women who do have 'mummy tummies'."

"So?" he inquired.

"So, it's not exactly sexy," she replied, embarrassed and hiding her face in the pillow. Of all things to chat about during 'pillow talk', how had they ended up discussing her 'mummy tummy'?

Realization dawned to the mental fog created by repeatedly satiated lust. "You're insecure about your body."

"Not my body," she mumbled into the pillow, "just my stomach. Like I said, it's not sexy. When you touch it, it reminds me of how it looks and I wonder how it must feel to you. When you touch the rest of my body, I feel sexy and wanted, but when you touch my tummy, I feel self-conscious and gross because you must think it's gross. Heck, I think it's gross. It's like a big sign to me that I've let myself go. I've tried to fix it. I've done those stupid tummy crunches, exercises, and everything. Then I read an article by a plastic surgeon and he said that what happens when a woman is pregnant is that the muscles of the stomach, also known as the six-pack, expand and pull apart and the only way to get rid of a 'mummy tummy' is to pull them back together with surgery or a tummy tuck. Even if I had the money for plastic surgery though, I don't know if I'd do it and one day, when I have more kids, it'll happen again anyway, so I have to live with it. I heard a mom in one of those antenatal classes speak of her pregnancy 'war scars' and how she's proud of it. Well, I'm proud of Amber, but that's one thing I'm not proud of - my tummy. I've let myself go and I'm only twenty-six years old."

He was astounded. For such an intelligent woman, she was sprouting a load of garbage. He didn't claim to understand what a woman went through during or after pregnancy, but her argument just didn't make sense to him. It defied logic. "Bree, look at me," Todd tugged at her.

Waving her arm at him to ward him off, she said, "no."

"Come on," he continued to tug, "look at me. I've already seen all of you, anyway, including your stomach. Come on," he repeated.

"Fine," she blurted out, then turned around and pulled the sheet up over her breasts feeling extremely self-conscious.

Todd shook his head then gently pulled the sheet down, exposing her stomach. He leaned down and kissed it, then laid his head on it and looked up at her. She seemed so insecure and vulnerable he wanted to scoop her up into his arms and comfort her. He'd do that but for now, he had to make a point.

"You turn me on," he stated.

"I get that," she rolled her eyes. "We've had sex four times in a few hours. That's pretty solid evidence of that."

"Good," he nodded, "we agree on that. What if I told you that all of you turns me on?"

"I'd say that you're lying through your teeth to be kind to me because the rest of me turns you on and you want to keep on having it."

"Jeesh, you never used to be such a moron," he groaned in frustration. "Pigheaded - yes, you've been that, but you weren't a pigheaded moron."

Bree narrowed her eyes at him and tried to kick him off her. "No wait," he stopped her holding her legs still with one arm. "You're a moron to think that every part of your body isn't a huge turn-on to me." When her legs stilled, he ventured on, "Do you know what turns me on the most?"

"What?" she asked.

"This," he said, leaning over to kiss her breasts, softly, tenderly.

Bree rolled her eyes again, "Go figure."

"And this," he went back to her stomach and kissed that too, softly, tenderly. At her skeptic stare, he continued, "Those are things on your body that have changed in the last seven years. I'm fascinated by them. They're signs of the miracle we created, of the miracle you carried and bore, the miracle that's our daughter." He looked at her stomach reverently, kissing it worshipfully. "And I think that's helluva sexy."

"You do?" Bree asked, voice small and eyes wide and filled with unshed tears.

"I do," Todd stated solemnly. "Let me show you just how much." He went on to do just that, lavishing attention on her breasts and stomach, lathing and licking them with devoted attention and showing her how much it turned him on until she started to relax and enjoy his administrations. Once she did, he made love to her, effectively wiping away her physical insecurities.

xxx

Bree's rumbling stomach stirred her from sleep. She was sprawled over Todd in the exact same position as when she'd first fallen asleep after his therapeutic lovemaking session. Slowly sliding out of the bed, she searched for the sweater she'd taken out of his closet drawer earlier before she'd become completely side-swept.

Sliding it over her head, she noted that the clock indicated nine in the morning though outside was still pitch dark. Amber would be awake now, as would her grandparents - time to call and check on them then make some breakfast. Tip-toeing around the clothes and sheets scattered over the floor so as to not wake him, she made her way down the stairs to the kitchen. After a hunt in the dark, she grinned at her foolishness and put the light on - he wouldn't wake up from the light down here when he was upstairs in bed. Shaking her head at herself, she acknowledged that she was more tired than she thought, but the activity to blame for her lack of sleep had been worth it.

Locating the phone, she made a quick call to the farm and spoke to her grandmother and Amber. Satisfied that they were okay and that Amber was well on her way to recovering from her nasty cold, Bree explained her sleep-over at Todd's. Her grandmother was embarrassed and mortified that she'd locked her granddaughter out the house and apologized profusely. She explained that Todd was still asleep and that he'd run her home later. As it was a Sunday, there wasn't any rush to do anything; it was the one day that things were kept laid-back in terms of farm chores so she didn't feel guilty about it. She felt a bit embarrassed chatting to her grandmother about a sleepover at a guy's place - even though the locked farmhouse gave her an excuse, so she was immensely relieved when no further questions were asked. Amber also seemed okay with it - assuming that a sleepover between her mother and father was natural.

Satisfied with the status quo, Bree replaced the phone on its stand and set about hunting around the kitchen to prepare breakfast. She found ingredients for a Spanish omelet. The man evidently liked his food. His fridge was stocked with a variety of ingredients not carried by the local stores. Like his coffee, he must've flown them in from Fairbanks, the largest metropolis near to them. Bree grabbed the eggs from the fridge and added them to the list of ingredients on the island countertop. The quiet of the winter morning lent itself to accentuating sounds around you so she was very much aware of Todd stirring, moving around the room, and turning the water on in the shower. She'd woken up to a few sensational surprises from him throughout the night, so she'd give him one this morning - one she felt very comfortable providing - a hot, filling, and tasty breakfast.

The mindless task of beating the eggs into a fluffy golden froth allowed her thoughts to wander. The night before had been sensational. She couldn't recall sex like that during their earlier courtship. The closest it came to was the last night they'd been together, the night she got pregnant.

Oh, God, she thought. What had she done? Accidentally burning her arm against the pan she was pouring the egg mixture into, she pulled back and knocked the pan straight off the stove. Stupefied by her realization, she watched in shock as the pan fell to the ground, spilling a mixture of egg, chorizo, and vegetables over the floor.

Cursing, she knelt down and started scraping the ingredients back into the pan, fumbling because she'd begun to shake. What the hell had she done?

"Bree," Todd called out from upstairs, "Are you okay?"

Bree heard his voice, but still numb, didn't respond. She didn't need to speak to him now, she needed time to think. Operating on auto-pilot, she managed to scoop the mixture off the floor and into the pan, and then dumped it next to the sink so she could run the burnt area on her arm under cold water.

"Bree?" Todd's voice broke through her reflections, startling her. Jumping in surprise, Bree knocked the pan to the ground and the ingredients spilled onto the floor again. She was going to dump them into the bin anyway, but the twice-spilled ingredients, a twice-made mistake, hit her hard. Sinking to the ground next to it, she sank down next to it, bursting into tears.

"What's wrong honey?" Todd asked, kneeling in front of her.

"We had sex, Todd," she bawled.

"I think we've ascertained that, Bree," Todd replied indulgently.

"No, that's not what I meant," she gasped in between sobs.

"What is it, Bree?" Todd inquired more firmly. The last time he'd seen her was a few hours ago and she'd seemed content. Now, he walks down to the kitchen to find her in pieces.

"We had sex," she reiterated.

"And?" he probed.

"And sex leads to complications and that's not something I was looking for?"

"Wait a minute," he said. "What complications? I'm not sure I'm on the same page with you."

"Complications that lead to the kind of life I was hoping to not have here in Devil's Peak. The kind of life that gets someone hurt. Amber," she blurted out. "Amber can't get hurt by this."

"Why would Amber get hurt by this?" he asked, confusion having replaced his own contentment.

"If we have a relationship and we break up, she'll be shattered," Bree explained. "We can't do that to her."

"What do you mean, 'if we have a relationship'? We are in a relationship. Not only are we her parents but we just made love - a number of times." Suddenly weary, Todd's voice held steel.

"We had sex, Todd,' Bree corrected. "Something only we know about. Let's keep it that way and not do it again."

For the second time since her return to Devil's Peak, Todd felt sucker-punched. Reeling from the shock due to the unexpected turn of events, he sat back and looked at her. She was a mess, shaking and sobbing as though her heart were breaking. "What's changed in the three hours since we made love to now?"

"Everything," Bree responded, unable to find the words to explain the many emotions flitting through her. With regret she realized that she'd found the man, she loved again and had to end it - for the sake of her daughter and herself.

"That's cold, Bree," Todd replied. "I realize that what we do can't impact Amber's happiness and I realize that she needs a stable home with both parents." He sighed in frustration, dragging his hands through his hair. Taking a breath, he confessed, "I planned to ask you to marry me. I can see a future with you and Amber here, in this house."

"So you want to marry me to have a whole and happy family," Bree caught on.

Todd flinched, confirming her suspicions. Infuriated, Bree bit out, "You sit there and admonish me for being concerned about the complications of sex when you used me, used sex for your own personal gain. You thought that if I slept with you, I'd marry you, didn't you?"

"It's not what you think," he interjected.

"No?" she cocked a brow at him. "Then what is it?" When he remained silent, she continued, "Do you love me Todd?"

"Of course, I love you," he responded. "We've known each other since we were kids. Except for the past seven years, you've always been a part of my life. And now, you're the mother of my child. That I love you is a given."

"That's not what I asked," Bree shook her head. "I asked if you loved me - me being Bree not me the mother of your child."

"Hell," Todd cursed. "I just answered the question." Todd had a bad feeling about where this was going, but just didn't get what she was going on about.

"No you didn't," Bree argued. "You said that you love me as a friend and as the mother of your child. I get that. I appreciate that. But, you didn't say that you love me for me. You love me as Bree regardless of everything that's happened in our past and present. I saw the crappy relationship my parents had - cold, distant familiarity bonded together by their warped sense of morality. That's what you're offering. We need to get married because we have a child and it's expected. That living together without love is okay because we're raising Amber together." Bree was panting from emotional frustration, shouting the words out at him. "Well, I want more than that. I deserve more than that. I want a man to love me, accept me, and cherish me - for me! A man who searches the room for me when he enters it, who feels the loss of my company when I'm not around

- I need a man who cannot bear the thought of not having me in his life. Are you that man, Todd?"

He stared at her wordlessly. Bree waited a moment, and then got up. "That answers my question. I'm going to shower, and then I'd appreciate it if you took me home."

He watched her get up and walk out of the kitchen. Rage replaced the shock and he roared, "That's fine. Walk away. Run away from the situation instead of facing it like an adult. Do what you did when you were pregnant with Amber. It's easier for you to be a coward."

"I'm not a coward," she turned back and yelled. "I'm not the one who left me. You did. You did it first. I was pregnant, hopeful that you'd come back from wherever and whatever it was that you were doing. That you'd come back and hold me, tell me things were going to be okay and that we'd get through it, but you didn't. I waited for you, Todd. I waited and hoped and you didn't come back. You're the coward."

"I didn't leave you," he argued. "You knew where I was going and what I was doing. For Pete's sake, I had just lost my father and gained the responsibility of looking after my siblings - financially and emotionally. I needed to make a plan and I was doing that while I was away. I wasn't doing drugs, living up life with whores on the dock. I wasn't doing anything but work, to save money to put food in my brother and sister's mouths!" He glared at her, angry that she'd judge him, hurt that she'd demand with so little empathy and understanding. "You're the one who left without saying a word. The first place I went to when I got back was the farmhouse. Did you know that?" At her flinch, he nodded. "I didn't think so. I came to you before I even said hello to my own brother and sister who I also hadn't seen for months. But, I didn't find you because you'd run away from facing me. I hadn't heard from you in years, not months - years," he repeated. "Then you walk back into my life, turn it upside down and just when I think we've worked things out, you want to walk out again."

"We didn't work a thing out," Bree countered. "We had sex, Todd, that's all. Hot sex but it was just sex nonetheless. That does not mean we're in a relationship. It does not mean that we've overcome our differences and it does not mean that I'll marry you so that you can fulfill your childhood fantasy of being part of a big, happy family."

Todd looked at her as though she'd slapped him. "You're right," he agreed in a cold voice. "There's nothing for us to talk about. Go," he pointed to the staircase, "go have your shower, and then I'll take you home. Running away seems to suit you better than I do."

Chapter 11

Bree sat by the lake, watching the activity around her. It was the first Sunday of summer and the place was teaming with people. Mothers sat on large, colorful picnic blankets, guarding the food against bugs and other critters nature had to offer. Ready to hand out sustenance to little fingers that needed it in between play. Fathers taught their children how to play catch, fly a kite, or swim in the expansive blue waters. The hollers, squeals, and laughter of children mingled lyrically with the sound of birdsong as nature had intended it to be.

Amber was playing with friends from school that she'd bumped into when they had arrived. Bree had diplomatically declined the invitations from the parents to sit with them, saying that she wanted to sit back and watch. That she needed the time to process the delights of her first summer back in Alaska. She knew that neither the words nor how she looked were convincing, but they would have to do. The last thing she felt like was being sociable.

Ever since the big argument with Todd, she'd felt lethargic and solitary, feelings reinforced by a deeper ache that seemed to permanently reside in her chest. If they'd truly loved each other, if they'd been a couple, she would've thought that her heart was breaking. But, her heart had already been broken once, when she'd fled Devil's Peak - pregnant and in disgrace, with no hope of seeing her lover again. She'd broken down and cried then; felt the pain of her heart ripping into pieces as the cold, harsh reality of teenage love gone wrong, sank in.

This feeling was different, less dramatic, but just as painful. It was the realization that she'd been disillusioned too often, that she'd allowed herself to fall to often and that she'd failed herself. She knew she needed to do something about it. She couldn't carry on the way she was - it wasn't fair to her grandparents or to Amber. She'd caught her grandparents sneaking worried looks at her and each other. When she did, she responded with cheerfulness, knowing that it came across as brittle and wouldn't alleviate their concern. Her feelings of self-defeat remained, like a heavy chain hanging around her neck, pulling her forward and down. She knew all of that, but she didn't know how to overcome it.

She didn't regret moving back to Alaska. It helped having her grandparents around and being part of a family again. Her grandparents seemed to thrive with the extra life in the farmhouse, having Amber and her to coddle and fret over. It was as though their energy was renewed. Amber, too, thrived here, having adapted to the extremes of Alaskan living naturally as though she'd been genetically made for it. Amber was doing well in school, had made new friends, loved the outdoor activities Alaska had to offer and mostly loved that she'd gone from being part of a two person family to a more extensive one with two grandparents and a father added.

As far as she went, there were a few things going well in her own life. Her career at the school was progressing in a positive direction. She'd worked hard and had earned the respect and trust of her colleagues and the principal. When she'd enhanced the children's aftercare program with a range of scheduled extra-curricular activities that nurtured and developed them creatively, physically, and mentally, the parents had begun to rave about it and her colleagues commended her. She now felt secure in her position at the school, no mean feat for a newly qualified teacher at her very first job. Thinking of her professional achievements lightened her heart a bit and Bree felt some of the ache dissipate.

"Hey Bree," a masculine voice interrupted her introspection.

Shielding her eyes against the sun with her hand, she looked up and saw Jack from The Lodge. "Hi," she returned the greeting.

"Mind if I sit?" he asked, indicating the spot on the blanket next to her.

She did mind, not really wanting the company, but couldn't say no without being rude, so she nodded her head instead. "Sure," she replied.

"I haven't seen you again at The Lodge," he began the conversation. "I guess Todd's been keeping you busy."

"Oh, Todd and I are not an item," she clarified. "We had dinner at The Lodge because Amber, my daughter," Bree waved an arm to where Amber was playing, "was sick so she couldn't go with her dad for the daddy -daughter dinner he had planned. Instead of cancelling the reservation, I filled in at the insistence of my grandmother and Amber of course."

"As you weren't a very willing participant," he said, looking at her, "I hope you enjoyed your dinner nonetheless."

"I wasn't unwilling," Bree clarified again. At his skeptical look, she laughed, her fist real laugh since the fight with Todd, "Oh, okay, I was unwilling. And yes, the dinner didn't disappoint. That's an amazing place you have there. You should feel really proud of yourself."

"Thank you and yes, I am happy that I've managed to keep it floating since most new businesses go under in the first two years and this was such a new concept for this part of Alaska. But," he waved his hand towards the many tourists intermixed with the locals at the lake, "as you can see, we've all embarked on a new journey in this town and it's paying off for all of us. Being local born and bred helped ease some of the resistance. I got the feeling that they were impressed by the money I made when I went to Silicone Valley and indulged my 'mad scheme' as they referred to it behind my back. Then, when I employed locals to help with everything that I could during the building phase, it chipped a bit off their block of resistance. Opening the restaurant and training locals to run it, sending them off for training in Paris, New York, and Anchorage helped some too. Bringing in fresh blood in the form of the beauty salon with a view to up-skilling two local girls had them nearly convinced. But, what convinced them was the increase in tourists visiting the town because of the niche accommodation The Lodge offers. It proved that I wouldn't steal away the other accommodation establishments' customers."

Bree watched him while he spoke. He was passionate, it animated him, and from what she heard, although he was a shrewd businessman, he'd kept the good of the community in mind. "I'm very impressed," she stated, warmly.

Jack actually blushed and waved the compliment away. "Oh no, I didn't say that to brag. My apologies, I get carried away sometimes and forget that it bores people."

"I didn't find that boring at all," she smiled at him. "Being back after a while, you see the changes and make assumptions about how they came about. It's good to hear it explained."

"I hear that you're doing great work at the school," he said, eyes twinkling with appreciation of the conversation. "In fact, I was wondering if I could pick your brain."

"Oh?" she inquired, wondering what on earth he was going on about.

"I have a mutually beneficial proposition to put forward to the school, but I don't want to go in blindly. It would help to be able to bounce my ideas off of someone who understands the school and the town. Would you be interested in helping?"

"That depends on what that help would entail," Bree answered, truthfully. "While Amber has settled down well, as a mom, I'm weary of getting too busy."

"For now," he said, "it would just be conversation. What do you say to brunch at The Lodge? I've got a meeting next Saturday, but am completely free the Saturday thereafter. I could come pick you up and we can have a meal and I can share my ideas with you - pick your brain?"

Bree had enjoyed their conversation. It had taken her mind nearly off Todd - nearly, not entirely. Maybe she needed a bit more of it. "Sure, that sounds great," she accepted, lips curving. "But don't worry about picking me up - seems like a lot of trouble. I'll just use Granddad's truck and meet you there." After they finalized the details of the meeting and said their goodbyes, she watched Jack walk off and she smiled to herself. The brunch idea did sound great and she found that she was looking forward to it.

xxx

While Bree was at the lake with Amber, the meddling busybodies of Devil's Creek were assembled at the Ramsay farmhouse to discuss the current state of affairs between Bree and Todd and to agree on the best approach they should take to resolve the situation. They called themselves the Devil's Peak Cares Association or DPC. They did a lot of good in the community. One Saturday a month, they sold pancakes at the local country market to fund their charity drives. They used the money to fund a number of youth programs, to provide frail care assistance to the elderly and they ran a bi-weekly soup kitchen. That was expected of them.

What wasn't expected, but appreciated was how they'd rallied in the past to raise funds for a local girl's wedding and given money and support to a family whose cancer-stricken young daughter needed a bone marrow transplant. More controversially, they'd made Brick Smith's life a living hell and ran him out of town after they'd found out that he was terrorizing his dear sweet wife and children. Though they'd vehemently deny it, they gave financial assistance to the woman and her brood to this day.

It was for all of these good works, and unselfish intentions that the town forgave them their meddling. For meddling, was there biggest, collective talent. Romantics at heart, they also made it their informal, though generally agreed upon mission, to bring together the young and old in love and holy matrimony.

"The polar bear swimming contest went well this year," Moira shared, running her eyes over the figures neatly tabled in the DPC's 'black book'. "We've raised enough money to continue for a few months with the programs we have and have a little left over to get those giant inflatables over from Fairbanks for the annual summer picnic."

"Let's not use the money for that," Mr. Stewart piped in. "As it is tourist season, let's apply to some of the local businesses to contribute towards getting it in, then we can bank the money for a rainy day - they always seem to creep up on us when we're broke and have no umbrellas."

"You're speaking like an outsider," Shelly chirped, drawing laughter from the others as she teased Mr. Stewart. "Alaskans never mind the weather. We deal with it. But, you do make a valid point. I could spring some cash from the boutique, use the opportunity for promotion. We'll probably have the inflatables for a while anyway as we'll have to fly them in. So, why don't we put them up in the town square after the annual picnic? That'll draw the tourists into town and give moms and dads a chance to shop and spend their money while the children play."

"Good idea," agreed Paula. "If that's the case, the grocery store could donate something too. We can round up some of the kids from the youth program and get them to watch over and entertain the little ones."

"Okay," interrupted Moira, "now that we have the picnic and the inflatables sorted, let's move onto Bree and Todd." Her eyes darted to the clock above the mantle-place. "It won't be long before she comes back."

"I'm stumped," Shelly said, empathically. "We've pulled out all the stops for them and they don't bite."

Mrs. Stewart's head bobbed vigorously in agreement. "They're a hard-headed couple, those two. In my day, you got together, got married, and dealt with whatever came your way. Nowadays, women want fairytales and men want superwoman. I don't know what the youth are on about."

Paula patted Mrs. Stewart's hand gently in consolation. "Now, now dear, don't upset yourself." Then looking at the other grim, flummoxed faces, she stated, "Sending Bree over with Todd's coffee had worked out so well. They'd ended up spending the whole day together and were in good spirits with each other for quite some time."

"In my day," interjected Mrs. Stewart, "the young people's parents had a conversation, and married them. The older generation knows what's best for the young ones. Now, that they have this freedom to choose, they keep buggering up." The others nodded out of courtesy and respect rather than agreement while Paula continued to pat Mrs. Stewart's hand.

"Do you remember Delilah and Rod?" Shelly hurriedly changed the subject with a random question. "We got them together quickly. We gave them an opportunity to get together alone, their lips locked, and that was the end of it."

"They locked more than their lips dear," Paula responded eliciting wicked grins and chuckles.

"My part went well too," added Mr. Stewart, bringing their attention back to the matter at hand. "Heck, I even played sick for a whole day so they could get locked up in the shed and from what mamma told me, they left the shed in a good way."

"It seemed to have gone wrong with my part," Moira offered, taking off her spectacles and folding it on the black book that sat on her lap, "forcing them to go to dinner together. It was just, too good an opportunity to miss, but maybe the lack of planning was where it went wrong. Since that night, they've been like icicles. You'd swear that we were still in winter it's so cold to be around them. And, what's more, Amber's a pretty perceptive child; she'll pick up on it eventually. The only thing keeping it from affecting her is their dedication to her that's making them put on a brave face in front of her."

Encouraged by the sympathetic looks thrown her way, Moira continued. "Maybe planning's the answer. You all planned your interventions to the last detail. This time around, probably because I'm so emotionally involved, I threw caution to the wind and acted spontaneously. We need another intervention and we need to plan it in detail."

The nods of agreement and ensuing plotting were abruptly stopped by Daniel Ramsay's booming voice as he entered the living room. "What you need," he looked Moira squarely in the eye, "is to leave them be, - you all need to back off."

Moira's head whipped back in surprise and Daniel felt a twinge of guilt. They'd been married for close to sixty years and she was still his darling girl, but sometimes her good intentions got in the way of her good mind. And, because she was as stubborn as he was, she wasn't open to hints and manipulation, so he needed to say it straight off, as hard as it was for him to be firm with her.

Taking a chair and placing it next to her, Daniel took Moira's hand and gently placed it in hers. She looked at him from lowered lids, eyes reflecting confusion and a bit of shame. Good, he thought, squeezing her hand in reassurance, there was a glimmer of guilt so there was hope to stop the 'Meddling Association' as he secretly called them.

He looked around at the unusually silent crowd, his friends, and neighbors, and said with as much feeling as he could muster, "Your intentions are good and I respect that. That you do so much good is honorable and kind. It makes you the best people I know."

The others in the room blushed or dipped their heads in embarrassment, because praise from the strong, stalwart Daniel did not come lightly or insincerely. Good, thought Daniel, things were going as he'd planned them to. "But sometimes, good intentions can lead to bad situations. And, although, you didn't mean for it to be so, that's what's happened with my granddaughter and that fine, young man. All was going as it should, as the natural way of things needed them to go. They were becoming accustomed to being a family, to being parents working together. Maybe they would've sorted things out and gotten back together and maybe they still will."

"But," the steel in his gaze stopped the conspiratorial gleams in their eyes, "if they get together, it'll take them to make to be turning that into reality. Not you. For I reckon that, you've made that harder. There's a rift between them now and no pushing them together is going to be fixing it. What's more is that I've never seen my granddaughter this unhappy before. I can take tears and tantrums but I can't take this martyred-type of happiness. That is killing her and it kills me to watch it. So, if you respect me and love me as I do all of you, then you'll grant me this one wish and not meddle this once. But knowing you, you can't sit back and just watch. So, I'll ask that instead of meddling, you lend them care and support, give them strength to heal from whatever happened and move on so maybe they can find that happiness we want for them by themselves."

Leaving them with that to chew on, Daniel leaned over and kissed his wife's forehead. "I better go check on my seedlings. I'll see you later, my darling." Moira grabbed his hand and squeezed it by way of apology. What he'd said had cut to the heart of things and because it wasn't what any of them had wanted to hear, that he'd pressed on because they'd needed to hear it, made him a brave man. The Irish in her didn't take to kindly to being ordered about and the squeeze was also meant to let him know that she forgave him for the set down.

Nodding in understanding, Daniel looked down at her and winked, before leaving them to the chaos that was bound to erupt upon his departure.

"Anyone for some more tea?" Shelly asked, breaking the ice.

"To hell with tea," grumbled Mrs. Stewart. "Moira, bring some of that Irish stuff you keep."

And like that, the atmosphere thawed. Drinking their 'Irish stuff', they smoothly, swiftly made a U-turn in the conversation and began merrily arguing and scheming on how to best support Todd and Bree.

Chapter 12

Her class dismissed and she was ready to go home, Bree walked down the hallway of the school to Amber's classroom to pick her up. The kids were restless - blame it on a Friday afternoon. Having the annual town picnic the next day didn't help temper down the excitement either. As adorable and understandable as that was, it had been tiring work to keep them calm enough to get through the day's lessons. Eventually, Bree had given up on the usual curriculum and had taken the kids outside to go bug-hunting and berry-picking from the wild, heavily bedecked bushes that sprang up like weeds during the Alaskan summer. The day hadn't then turned out to be a waste as the children received a very practical biology lesson under the open sky.

Outside Amber's class, waiting with the other parents of children who did not live on the bus routes, was her grandmother. "Hi gran," she said, kissing her cheek in greeting. "What brings you here?"

"I was in town," Moira explained, "and finished what I was doing earlier than expected. So I thought I'd pop by and take Amber out for a treat - some Gran and Amber special time."

"That's very sweet of you," Bree beamed. "I'm sure Amber will love it."

"Oh, I'll love it too," Moira said smiling.

"Hi Amber," Bree waved her daughter over as she exited her classroom. It was really cute that Amber insisted that her mother call her by name whilst at school and not by a term of endearment. Bree observed her daughter hug another girl, who was fast becoming her best friend, before heading towards them. It wasn't long ago that they were in Columbus and Amber ran towards her mom whenever she spotted her after school. Feeling the twinge of time gone by, Amber relished the fact that her little girl was growing up and establishing real roots in Devil's Peak.

"Hi Mom, hi grandma," Amber scurried over and gave them each a peck on the cheek. "Why are you both here?"

"I've got a surprise for you," Moira leaned down and whispered conspiratorially in Amber's ears. Bree watched Amber's eyes pop wide then glisten with excitement at the treats her grandmother was promising.

"I'll leave the two of you then to go and enjoy yourselves. I'll see you back home later," Bree said. "I'll start dinner in the meantime. Should I tell granddad that you'll be a while?"

"No need for that dear," her grandmother patted her hand. "Granddad knows what we're doing? It's funny how things seem to just fall into place this morning. I got dinner done this morning so no need for you to see to it. And then when I was in town earlier, I saw Shelly. I told her of my plans to take Amber out and she said she'd do the same and come and get you. Something about not seeing you often enough lately - I think she misses you. In fact," Moira nodded towards the tall, beautiful woman walking down the hallway, "looks like she's here. So, the only thing you have to do is go and enjoy yourself."

Bree took a moment to watch Amber skip hand in hand with her grandmother, eagerly chattering away. She walked towards Shelly and gave her a big hug. "I'm a bad friend, Shelly," Bree said. "I've been so caught up in myself lately that I've completely neglected you."

Shelly shrugged it away, "No worries, hun, as long as you make it up to me today. I've got stacks of interesting things planned for us. That's all I want for my birthday."

Bree flinched inwardly. Goodness, she'd been so self-obsessed that she'd completely forgotten her best friend's birthday. Smiling at Shelly, she swore to herself that she'd make it up to her and fall in with whatever plans she had. "Then let's go. Your birthday, your party, and your rules."

"Music to a girl's ears," Shelly smiled back and they walked out to the car arm in arm like they had as teenagers.

xxx

"What are we doing here?" Bree asked. They had parked in front of the medical center. "Are you sick?" Bree scanned Shelly worriedly, looking for signs of ill health.

"Nope," replied Shelly, "just a check-up. Come with me, it won't take long."

Bree followed Shelly still concerned, but ready to support her friend.

"Shelly Adams and Bree Tanner Ramsay to see Dr. Dimitrov," Shelly informed the receptionist.

"Her last appointment cancelled unexpectedly so she's ready to see you," the receptionist stated. "Why don't you two go on through? It's the second to the last door on the right."

The room they entered was not the usual doctor's abode. One corner looked like it belonged in a restaurant play area and was set up with loads of toys, a children's boxing bag, sandpit, and loads of dolls.

There was even a kiddies' table and chairs with crayons and blank paper to draw on. This doctor must love kids, Bree thought. Maybe this was a pediatrician. But why would Shelly need one? There was no need for her to be here - Bree's eyebrows shot up - unless Shelly was pregnant.

The other side of the room held an informal lounging area with chairs facing each other. By the window was a traditional desk and chair at which sat a middle-aged woman with a welcoming smile. The woman got up and came around the desk to greet them, "Hi Bree, Shelly, welcome. Pleased to meet you, I'm Doctor Roz."

"Hi," they both replied in unison and sat down at the chairs the doctor waved them towards.

"So, what brings you here?" Doctor Roz asked.

"Well, I'm here for my friend, Bree," Shelly began.

Bree looked at Shelly in surprise. "I'm not sick," she said.

Shelly looked at Bree, guilt written all over her face and took her hands in hers. "I know you're not sick. Doctor Roz is not a GP, she's a psychologist."

Startled, Bree felt trapped, manipulated, and angry. Shelly stopped the tirade that Bree was about to let out with an indication of her hand. "Wait. Hear me out. Please," Shelly begged.

"You've been down now for months," Shelly continued. "You won't talk about it and in fact, you've been avoiding, not only, my company, but everyone's company for just as long. You're living in your own world and while I'd be okay with that if it made you happy, you're not happy. In fact, you're downright miserable. You've never been vain, but you're even letting yourself go."

When Bree opened her mouth to speak, Shelly stopped her again, "For the sake of our friendship and for your own sake, here me out please?"

"For the sake of our long history together and because I love you, I'll hear you out before I strangle you," Bree promised furiously.

Shelly nodded and hurried on, not wanting Bree to change her mind. "You hardly eat, so you've lost a lot of weight. You dress like a bag lady and when do the last time you did your hair or put make-up on. You're twenty-five years old, not seventy-five. You only speak when spoken to and you don't go out. Like I said, I hardly see you and when I do it's by chance. Your grandparents say that you're like that at home too. Once Amber's gone to bed, you go and shut yourself up in your room."

"I've just moved back to Alaska, Shelly, with a young child in tow," Bree bit out. "That's bound to wear anyone out. Why should I be any different?"

"I'd buy that if you'd been here for just a month or two, but you've been here for just over six months. That's a long enough time to adjust, especially with all the support you have, and because you grew up here so nearly everything is familiar to you." Shelly took a heartbeat of a moment to catch her breath before she continued making her case. "I realized that you weren't yourself when I stopped by your grandparent's house last month and you were sleeping. Amber and your grandparents were sitting in the kitchen eating your gran's birthday cake. Apparently, you went to bed after dinner with a headache. They were worried about you, but you'd even apparently forgotten about your gran's birthday. That is so unlike you that I began to worry. The Bree I grew up with always had a plan for anyone's special day. We even called you Birthday Girl because you were always planning outrageous events to celebrate people's birthdays. You loved it - it's why I thought you'd eventually become a party planner. Then, today, you even forgot mine." Shelly's eyes filled with tears.

Feeling like a wretch, Bree leaned over and hugged her friend, "I'm sorry, hun; I didn't mean to forget your birthday. My head's just been full of stuff lately."

"I know," sniffed Shelly, "and it's not the birthday I'm crying about. Stuff the birthday! I'll have more. I'm worried about you. It broke my heart when you left Devil's Peak and when you came back, I was super-excited. I had my Bree back. You're more than just a friend, Bree. I've known you since I was five year's old. To me, you're the sister I never had. I'm worried about you because I love you and I can't stand to see you in pain anymore. But, as much as I love you, I also know that you can be an idiot when you get pig-headed about something. So, this is my way of making you do something to get better and give me my Bree back. This is the only birthday present I want. In fact, stay and give Doctor Roz a chance and you never have to give me another present again. I'd much rather have you."

Bree looked at Shelly through watery eyes. "My God, I'm a mess. I forgot gran's birthday, I forgot your birthday and you're right, I have been avoiding everyone. It's just so hard, you know, to pretend that everything's okay."

Doctor Roz stepped into the conversation. "What it sounds like to me, Bree, is that you're experiencing a depressive episode or what people simply call depression. It is a proper medical condition and more common than you realize. I can help you get back up on your feet and feel better. Would you like to stay and talk to me about it? You can try it out today, hear what I have to recommend and then decide if you'll come back. Does that work for you?"

Bree cast a glance at Shelly's hopeful glance, and then looked at Doctor Roz and nodded. "Okay, I'll give it a shot."

Breathing a sigh of relief, Shelly hugged her friend and got up to leave the room. I'll be waiting outside when you're done.

xxx

"So, how did it go?" Shelly asked as they got back into the car.

"It went well," Bree answered though her eyes that were a bit puffy from crying. "Shelly," Bree said facing her friend, "thank you for what you've done. I was mad as hell at first when I realized you'd tricked me, but it was right. I needed to see Doctor Roz."

"My pleasure," Shelly beamed at Bree through misty eyes. "What did she say?"

"She diagnosed me with a clinical episode of depression," Bree responded. "That doesn't mean that I'm depressed and need to go on medication for the rest of my life. In fact, I didn't want to go onto the medication she prescribed for three months, but she explained what happens in the brain when someone is depressed and how the medication helps restore balance to the brain's chemistry. We think the depression was caused by what happened after I got pregnant." Bree shrugged, "You know, my parents' reaction, leaving town, doing it alone and then coming back and the fight with Todd. Apparently all of that causes a shock to the system and enough of it creates a chemical imbalance - hence the depression."

"So, you'll take the meds?" Shelly inquired, looking at the script in Bree's hands.

"I'll take the meds," Bree nodded, "but only for three months and then we'll reassess. I'm going to begin doing other stuff that'll help speed recovery too and I've worked out a program of sorts with

Doctor Roz. I'll ask gran to pick Amber up from school on Fridays so that I can continue therapy with Doctor Roz, I'm going to start exercising and I'm going to go on a healthy eating plan. I've got a list of food here that help, which Doctor Roz recommended."

"I'm so proud of you," Shelly beamed at Bree, unclicking her seatbelt to lean over and hug her. "And anything you need, just call. I'm here for you. In fact, I never get to spend time with my niece between Todd and your grandparents, so Friday's are mine. I'll pick her up from school and take her to the boutique and when we're not busy, the manager can run the place and we can do girly things. It'll be fun."

"You're the best friend anyone could ever ask for," Bree responded with a watery smile. "Thank you."

xxx

After they'd filled the prescription for her medication, Bree and Shelly strolled arm in arm down the town's main street.

"Shelly," Bree stopped her friend. "Do you think we could go to the hair salon?"

"Sure," Shelly nodded, "but first, we need to go in there." Shelly pointed to the local gym, which to Bree could just as well have been a house of horrors.

Bree grimaced, "I was thinking of exercise more along the lines of long walks in the woods, swimming in the lake and so on. Besides, I have Amber with me when I get out of school."

"That's not a problem," Shelly shook her head. "I'm joining too and we are both going to get our asses so tight that no man is going to be able to look straight after we pass them by. And, they've got an excellent kiddies' care facility and kiddies' exercise program that Amber can join. What's more, because I'm part of DPC and so is your gran, we both get discounted rates."

Bree shrugged, "Okay, I like that Amber can join in and we'll get to see each other more often. So, yeah, let's do this."

Moments later, gym membership cards in their wallets, and feeling lighter of heart, they stepped into the hair salon. "So, hun," Shelly prompted, "you asked to come here so go forth and do."

"Nope," Bree grinned back wickedly. "We'll both go forth and do. You've always wanted to be a blonde and I've always wanted your black hair, so that's what we're doing."

"Don't you think that's a bit drastic?" Shelly asked.

"Sure," Bree shrugged nonchalantly, "but what good is a change without a kick-ass haircut."

"Well, you said it," Shelly caved and they made their way to the waiting chairs of future hair-shocked bliss.

Chapter 13

They had their hair done and despite the denied trepidation that they'd felt, they admitted that they looked hot, in the way that close girlfriends did. The black color predictably made Bree's skin look pale, but it also brought out the pink in her cheeks and blue in her eyes so that the end result was ethereal rather than odd. Tall, bronzed Shelly looked like an Amazon Goddess ready to crack a whip and break hearts while she was at it.

Hair done and a mountain of shopping bags filled with makeup and clothing, they merrily made their way to the diner for a quick coffee and wild berry pie to end the day off with. After placing their order, Shelly slid an envelope across the table to Bree. "Your grandmother asked me to give this to you. And yes, it was all planned - her taking Amber out, me taking you to Doctor Roz. You're not mad, are you?"

"At you all meddling in my life?" Bree asked, and then grinned. "No. I'm not mad. I should be, but I feel better today than I have in months so I can't be mad at you."

Phew! Shelly breathed a sigh of relief. "Okay, so open it," she prompted. "I've been carrying that around with me all afternoon and you know how much I hate waiting for surprises like you do."

Giggling, Bree slit open the envelope and took out a homemade card and a note. She read the note first and slid the card to Shelly, thinking that Amber had made her a birthday card. The note read:

"Our dearest Bree, Ever since you came into our lives, you've given us nothing but joy. The hardest thing we've had to do was watch you suffer as life continued to throw challenges at you. But, we want you

to know that you've done us proud in the way that you've met those challenges head on. You've grown from our darling little girl into a fine, strong woman with a beautiful heart. You've given us so much and for that, we wanted to, in a small way, say thank you.

We've made arrangements at that fancy place, The Lodge, for Shelly and you to spend the night. They'll treat you to a dinner and give you loads of those fancy spa things. Then, you girls can go and gossip away in a room there for the night like you used to when you had sleepovers. Tomorrow morning you'll have a huge breakfast because you're getting a bit too skinny and we're worried about that and we'll see you later for the town's picnic.

I know it sounds like we're managing and if we're honest, we'd admit that we are. But, we'll use a grandparent's prerogative here and ask you to indulge us instead. Let us say thank you and show you our love.

All our love and kisses,

Gran and Granddad

Both tearful, Bree and Shelly looked up at each other, smiled tentatively, and swapped letters. The card that Amber drew was beautiful, kind, and heart-breaking.

"Mom, Get better soon. See you tomorrow. Love, Amber"

"I've already made up my mind to get better, Shelly," Bree said to her friend while they both touched tissues to the corners of their eyes. "But, if I ever needed motivation to get my butt into gear and get over myself, then Amber's card was it."

Chapter 14

Hot heels, make-up, and killer dresses on, Bree and Shelly stepped into the local bar cum night club, ready to celebrate Shelly's birthday and Bree's metamorphosis, as they were referring to it. Since the influx of tourists, the bar had turned, seeing a gap in the market, transformed into a night club on Friday and Saturday nights during the in-season. The change had become so popular with locals that the bar now permanently functioned, on those two nights, as a place where locals could eat, have a drink and socialize or dance to their heart's content.

As it was just before summer vacation, tourists had begun to flock to the wild of Alaska. The place was packed. Moving through the hordes of bodies standing around tables, sitting at the bar and picking at baskets of fried delights, they made their way to a table in the corner.

Hyped up in the hotel and buzzing after an emotional roller-coaster of a day, the two of them decided to call a bunch of friends of high school to meet them there.

"Now I know what took you so long," Kristine drawled, "you both look sensational. Happy birthday, Shelly." Kristine had been in the cheerleading squad with them, along with Alice, Megan and Kelly. They excitement was palpable. When they got together a good time was guaranteed - just like in high school. Since then four out of the group of friends had gotten married and had children, so a girls' night out was a rare occurrence. It took very little convincing from Bree and Shelly to get them out of their homes and into the night club.

After rounds of hugs and a few rounds of drinks - Bree remembered her one and only drunken night and stuck to soft drinks - the group of girls made their way to the dance floor, merrily oblivious to the admiring glances they were getting from other patrons. Shelly had bribed the DJ to play a few tracks from their senior year and the women let it rip, dancing their old moves, and not caring what anyone thought. They felt the sense of freedom that only dancing without a care can give.

Before sitting back at the table with the others, Bree offered to go fill their drinks; the bar was so packed that they were having to wait at least a half an hour before a waitress could come and take their order. She found a gap at the bar counter and squeezed herself into it. Tapping her fingers against the bar counter, she waited for her turn to give her order.

"Excuse me ma'am," a familiar voice said to the back of her head as he reached for the beer offered to him by the barman.

"Todd," she turned around and faced him.

She had the satisfaction of seeing Todd do a double-take, give her a once-over (seemingly enjoying it) then look back at her in shock. "Bree?" he asked.

"The one and the same," she replied.

"Definitely Bree," he said, his eyes automatically exploring the curves hidden beneath the flaming hot, midnight blue dress that made her eyes pop. "But not the same," he added. "You dyed your hair," he stated the obvious.

"Yes," she said, twirling her hair around her fingers.

"Looks good on you," he said sounding less friendly and more forcibly polite, the shock of the change wearing off and reality setting back into place. "Look, I gotta go. I'll see you tomorrow when I pick Amber up for the picnic."

"Actually," Bree stopped him, "I won't be at home tomorrow morning. I'm staying over at The Lodge. But, I do need to speak to you - it's important."

"Oh," Todd looked at her in surprise for the second time that night, "are you and Jack together then?"

Bree shook her head in confusion. "What? You think that…Jack and I?" She shook her head again to indicate no. "I'm not staying over with Jack. Shelly and I are staying there because it's her birthday today. We're celebrating. That's why I'm back there with the girls."

Todd swung his head around and waved at the table of old high school friends. "I see," he stated. "I thought that was what you wanted to chat about - that you and Jack are an item. He does have the hots for you - always did."

"He so does not," retorted Bree. "And, even if he did, I'm not going down that road, not right now."

"Ah, yes," Todd nodded, "I recall having this conversation with you before." He tipped his head at her. "See you tomorrow then."

"Wait, Todd," Bree stopped him with a hand on his arm. "I really do need to speak with you and I'd rather you hear what I've got to say from me directly and soon."

"Is something wrong?" He came closer, looking worried. "Is Amber alright?"

"Amber's fine," she confirmed, "And nothing's wrong now. Something was, but it's getting sorted out."

He lifted a brow at the cryptic comment. Bree clarified, "This isn't the place to talk about it - sorry - that's why I'm not blurting it out."

"Okay, but it sounds important," he acknowledged. "If you and Shelly are staying over at The Lodge then you'll probably have breakfast there. Why don't I come around and we could grab a coffee and chat. Will that work?"

"That'll be fine," she replied. "Thank you."

"No problem, Bree. See you tomorrow."

XXX

"Oh honey," Shelly said empathically when they got back to the hotel room, "you got it bad?"

"Got what bad?" Bree asked.

Shelly didn't respond, she just quirked a brow before going into the bathroom to shower and change. Bree waited for Shelly to shower, knowing from their shared childhood that she'd be quick.

Minutes later, Bree was joined by Shelly. Sitting opposite each other, feet curled beneath their legs on the over-sized sofas, ready for a good gossip of the night's events. Shelly approached the subject again. "How long have you been back in love with Todd?"

Bree knew that she couldn't fool her best friend and on this new journey of self-improvement, being honest with Shelly but more importantly being honest with herself, had to start happening. "I could say that I fell in love again once we started spending time with each other. Or I could say that it happened when we first kissed again at the New Year's dance or when we made love again. But, if I had to be truthful, I'd say that I don't ever think that I've not been in love with him. It seems that I may have left Devil's Peak with a baby growing inside of me, but I left the part of my heart that loved a man behind."

"Oh, hun," Shelly reached out and squeezed Bree's hand. "This calls for more wine. I noticed that you haven't had any tonight. Coffee?"

"No thanks, I'll make some tea instead; a good, soothing chamomile," Bree replied. Beverages in hand, Shelly probed, "So you guys slept together again?"

"Yes," Bree nodded, "many times and just before the fight that split us apart for good. Since then, we see each other when he comes over to visit Amber, when I drop Amber off at his place or if we pass each other by in town. That's it. We're polite and greet each other, but we don't speak, not really."

"And I'm guessing that it hurts?" Shelly asked.

"Like hell," Bree chuckled through her tears. "The thing is that we both stuffed up. That night, after we made love, we had a huge fight. We said things, I think, to deliberately hurt each other. Things about the past, about what we thought our future was going to be like together."

"Let me guess," Shelly interjected. "You raked him over the coals for not contacting him while he was gone after his daddy's death and leaving you alone to face your parents with an unexpected pregnancy. And he blamed you for running away and leaving him."

"How did you know?" asked Bree, impressed by Shelly's perceptiveness.

"Oh, I think it's about time the two of you got into an honest shouting match," she explained. "What you guys went through wasn't great. It sucked. But, the way you both handled it sucked even more."

"I did the best that I could Shelly and so did he," Bree muttered in defense.

"I don't doubt that you did, honey," Shelly said gently. "But, the truth is that there's no recipe for handling situations such as yours or Todd's. And, that is what I think the problem is. The two of you have always been so busy being strong - him because of his past with his crappy parents and you because your own crappy parents forced you to be strong - like a robot - so that you never made any mistakes. Then you go and make one of the biggest mistakes of all, according to them, - a teenage pregnancy. It was bound to cause waves. But, instead of crashing against them, you both rode the waves that were sent your way."

Shelly took a sip of wine, mulled over it while studying her friend. Bree was listening, as evident by her chewing her bottom lip - that was good. Shelly needed her to listen. "I'm saying that you're not robots but you acted like one. Now, I'm no Doctor Roz, but if people go through things, they gotta cry, gotta rant and rave a bit and get it out of their systems. That's normal. You didn't even cry and I've never seen Todd cry and I've known him for as long as I've known you and nearly as well. You just bury whatever is really brewing inside and get on with things. Eventually though, things catch up to you. I reckon that the big fight, as you call it, was things catching up to you both. And, look where you are now. Again, you're both moving on with things."

They each sat in silence digesting what was said, nursing their drinks. "Okay," Bree said eventually, "that was deep."

It was such a simple evaluation of what Shelly had said that they both burst into laughter. After a few more minutes of uncontrolled laughter, Bree continued, wiping tears evoked by their guffaws from her eyes, "You're right though. The more I think about it - what you said and the conversation with Doctor Roz - the more I realize that while Todd and I had to do what we had to, we both put ourselves on the back-burner and our emotions were the first parts of us that went there."

"Amen to that," Shelly held up her glass in salute. "So what are you going to do about how you feel for him?"

"What can I do?" Bree shrugged. "I may have feelings for him, but I don't think they're returned."

Shelly grunted in frustration. "For Pete's sake, Bree, how can someone so intelligent be so darned blind."

"What do you mean?" Bree blinked at Shelly, baffled.

"I saw him talking to you tonight," Shelly offered. "First there was lust - the guy couldn't take his eyes off of you. But, given that we're looking pretty hot tonight, that was kinda expected."

Bree rolled her eyes and waved a hand to indicate that Shelly should continue. Todd had lusted after her tonight? Darn, she hadn't even noticed that!

"But then," Shelly went on, "I saw care and concern. I don't know what you guys were talking about, but the man looked like he wanted to take you into his arms and keep you safe. I don't know about you, but that's a good thing to have in a partner."

"I didn't notice that," Bree stated.

Now it was Shelly's turn to do an eye roll, "Of course, you didn't. You were too busy doing some lusting yourself. And, I got an insecure, nervous vibe from you - like you didn't know what to expect."

"Are you sure you're not working with Doctor Roz, Shelly?" Bree inquired. "I'm pretty impressed by your perceptiveness."

"I sell expensive clothing to high-end tourists mostly in rural Alaska," Shelly stated factually. "How do you think I manage to do that? It's all about figuring out what people desire and giving it to them."

Bree held up her teacup in salute then ventured, "So what do you think I should do?"

"Nope," Shelly shook her head, "you're not getting off that easy. What do you think you should do about it? Do you want to be with him?"

"Oh yes," Bree answered.

"I've already established for you that he's giving off the same vibe," Shelly responded. "So, now you gotta answer for yourself, how do you get him back?"

"Okay, I get it," Bree acknowledged her friend's advice. "I have some seducing to do, or courting first at least."

"Yes," agreed Shelly, "sort through your crap with each other before hitting the sack this time around."

Bree nodded, "Yes, like I told him the night of the big fight, it's not just about sex."

"Honey," Shelly chuckled, "you told him that? After making love to him?"

Bree smiled sheepishly, "Five times."

"Oh my word, no wonder the man was furious," Shelly chuckled. "You bruised his ego. Honey, when men sleep with you, they think it's just sex but you're not allowed to. They think that to you it must be the most earth-shattering, wonderful experience of your life that elevates them to the level of a demi-God."

Bree looked indulgently at Shelly. One day, she was going to get Shelly to tell her what had made her become so cynical. "It wasn't just sex, though, Shelly. I don't think for either of us because he did get pretty angry at me when I said it. But, what I agree with you about is that sex, lovemaking, whatever you want to call it, is not going to solve our problems. I said as much that night and the words were right, are right even now, but my intentions behind them are different." At Shelly's look of confusion, she explained. "That night I said it because I'd panicked, because I remembered what had happened after the last time we'd slept together. Now, I'm saying it because I believe that we have to talk things through, agree to make this work between us before we sleep together again."

"Well, good luck with that, honey," Shelly, chirped. "The two of you looked about ready to explode with sexual frustration tonight. But, I get what you're saying and can't say that I disagree with your thinking. I just don't know how practical that's going to be. You know, Bree, sex is good, fun, and normal, so you shouldn't repress those feelings either. Just learn to have a bit more balance."

Bree cocked her head, considering. "Makes sense and I admit to a bit of relief. Well, a whole lot of relief, really," Bree grinned, wickedly. "But, we're talking as though Todd's going to be agreeable about us getting back together. We don't know if things will work out that way."

"Trust me," Shelly stated firmly, "that man wants you in his bed and his heart. I sell high fashion, remember." They chuckled at the odd rightness of that statement.

Feeling more hopeful, Bree hugged Shelly in thanks. "I get it. You're telling me to go for it with him - to win him back."

"I said no such thing," Shelly replied stiffly, "far be it from to meddle."

Grinning widely, because Shelly was a relentless meddler and always had been, Bree went to have a long soak in a hot, fragrant bath. She'd been through a lot that day and she figured she deserved it. Finally.

Chapter 15

They elected to have breakfast in their room the next morning so that they could raid the meager supply of clothing they'd brought in preparation for Bree's discussion with Todd. Thankfully, she'd bought a new pair of jeans and a smart casual sweater to wear to the town's picnic because nothing Shelly had fit her figure or her complexion.

"This'll have to do." Bree studied the dark blue denim and black light-knit sweater. "It seems a bit boring though."

"Nothing, the right accessories can't fix," Shelly offered, quizzically studying Bree in the mirror from behind. "And fortunately for you, short pants, they're one size fits all."

Bree picked up the nearby cushion off a chair and threw it at Shelly. "Yes, giraffe is so last season."

"Cow," Shelly retorted mockingly, sending them into more giggles.

Moments later, when reception called to notify her that Todd was waiting in the lobby, Bree did another quick study. With the added make-up, lip gloss, and jewelry, she looked good and ready for battle. She was going to win this man over once and for all - starting today.

With each step taken down the elegant stairs, Bree became more and more nervous. Hands clammy, she grabbed the balustrade, to steady herself. Get a grip Bree, she admonished, where is all your talk of fighting and courage. At the end of the landing, she spotted Todd, leafing through an outdoors magazine while lounging in the ample sofa. The sofa might be large but tall and masculine; Todd didn't allow it to dwarf him.

Like her, he was dressed in denim and a sweater; casual summer picnic wear, very unlike the smart, sophisticated look he sported when they'd last been together at The Lodge. Bree didn't care what he wore; he looked good in just about anything. Just as she got to the landing, he looked up and smiled at her in greeting and Bree felt a million fluttering wings of butterflies in her tummy.

Glancing around the lobby, she noted that it was a hive of activity as people prepared to set off for their day's planned activities. Many of them were dressed in jeans, shorts, and sweaters and carrying picnic blankets. Bree's lips curved, if the picnic drew in a good number of tourists, it would be added confirmation that the town was well on its way to establishing its place on the Alaskan tourism map. Not to mention that her gran would be thrilled as the chairperson of the Devil's Peak Cares Association. Her gran and fellow association members had been planning the picnic for months, which was an added reason to be grateful for her grandparents' gift of the room. With both Bree and Shelly out of the picture to help pitch in with the last-minute arrangements and her granddad no doubt looking after Amber, her gran must've had her hands full. Bree made a mental note to get her grandparents a gift to say thanks and to give them the night and the next day off from farm and house work. They all normally pitched in and did their bit, but they deserved to put their feet up. She'd rope in Shelly and they'd turn it into a game for Amber; have some fun doing work.

Todd met her in the middle of the lobby by a large table bearing an oversized arrangement of flowers. "Hi," she said, "thanks for coming. I really appreciate it, especially since the shop must be busy."

"I closed for today," Todd shrugged. "I thought that if I did, it would give the picnic a fair shot, so no problem. Wanna get some coffee?"

Bree peered past his shoulder into the exceptionally busy entrance of the dining room. Children ran in and out of the room, babies cried from beyond and the clinking sound of crockery and cutlery intermingled with excited breakfast chatter made it noisy. It was a great place to go if you wanted to get into a vacation mood but not one for a private, serious conversation.

"Uh… it's kinda loud in there," Bree stated. "If you want coffee, I could go and ask if they could bring us some out to the veranda instead? There are tables and chairs out there that we could sit at."

"I'm okay," Todd replied. "You know that I'm a bit of a coffee snob and I've already had a few cups this morning. The ads for this place said that it had 'beautiful gardens.' Should we go for a walk and see if Jack has put his money where his mouth is?"

A bit jealous, aren't we, Bree thought satisfactorily. "The gardens would be fine. And from what I've seen, I'm sure that Jack's delivered on his promise." Bree couldn't resist stoking that flame. A little bit of jealousy wouldn't hurt. At least it indicated that he was feeling something!

After consulting reception on the allocation of the gardens, they navigated the outside of the hotel, around the lake and found a rather unimpressive sign stating, "Gardens." Bree and Todd looked at each other and grinned. "Delivering on his promise, you said?" Todd quirked a brow at her jokingly.

Bree shrugged, "Let's go find a bench, assuming that this piece of forest has one."

"You noticed that did you?" Todd asked.

"Yes," replied Bree. "It's very clever of Jack if you think about it. The locals wouldn't come here for a walk in the gardens. We'd just walk around the forests surrounding the town. But folk who aren't from here wouldn't necessarily know better, so I imagine that to them, this would be spectacular."

Todd looked around, noticing the lush green leaves of the trees, the wild berry trees bearing colorful abundance of fruit, heard the birds chirp in chorus. "I see what you mean and even though it's what we're used to, if you stop and think about it, it is pretty impressive."

"Well you know," Bree, stated, "you explore our surroundings as a career. A pretty good career if you ask me."

Todd inclined his head in acknowledgement of the compliment, "thank you. And there's you a bench." He pointed towards a fallen log that lay along the man-made path.

"So," he began, turning around to face her as she seated herself next to him on the log, "what did you want to talk to me about?"

This close to his face, Bree noticed that he looked tired and drawn, as though he wasn't getting much sleep. It tugged at her heart and she resisted the urge to wrap her arms around him, ask him about it, and comfort him.

Taking a breath to steal a moment and gather her thoughts, she looked in front of herself and blurted out, "I went to see Doctor Roz on Friday."

"Are you ill?" Todd asked, his voice laced with concern.

"No," Bree shook her head, "she's not a medical doctor, and she's a psychologist."

"Oh," Todd relaxed and waited for her to continue.

"It was Shelly and my gran's idea," she explained, twining the hem of her sweater around her fingers. "I'd been feeling down and neglecting myself and those around me. They noticed and sprung an intervention on me. Unfortunately, Amber picked up on it."

That confession made Todd sit up straighter. "Not in a way that I think harmed her," Bree quickly spelled out, "but she'd picked up on something and thought I was sick. I wanted you to know that because we're parents together and whatever affects Amber, however little it is, you deserve to know."

"Thank you for telling me," Todd said sincerely. "It means that you trust me as a parent and I appreciate that. But are you okay?"

"I'm much better now," Bree affirmed. "Doctor Roz diagnosed me with an episode of depression, which means that it's not permanent and with the right treatment such as medication and a healthy lifestyle, I should be okay in a few months and able to go off the medication. I'll also be going for weekly therapy sessions with Doctor Roz."

"To be honest," Bree confessed, "I think that I just needed the kick in my behind to pull myself together. I know that it sounds optimistic and because of that, and because I don't want to take chances and get sucked into that black hole again, I'm going to follow the treatment to the letter. But, my grandparents and Shelly have been great. Even Amber," Bree took out Amber's card and her grandparent's letter and handed it to him. Nervous again, she chattered on, "So, all will work out in the end. It's already better. I actually went from not wanting to see anyone to having a blast last night."

Todd folded the card and letter and returned it to her, then scooted over and pulled her into a hug. Bree was so startled that she didn't know how to react and remained frozen in his arms. Pulling away, she looked up at him quizzically.

His arm around her shoulders, he looked at her, sincere concern showing in his expression, "Regardless of all that's gone wrong in our relationship, there was a lot of right too. And, regardless of us having a daughter together, you were my friend for a very long time. I'll always care for you Bree. I can't ignore the fact that you were a major part of my life before and will be going forward. So, I'm sorry for what you've been going through and I can't help but feel as though this mess we got ourselves into helped put you there. I'm not taking the blame entirely because I feel that there's enough for both of us, but I'm sorry for my part in it and want you to know, as the mother of my child and as my friend, if you need anything, I'll be there."

Bree looked up at him in surprise, touched by how easily he uttered those words and meant them. Then again, Todd had always been quick to rescue and help out; it was how he was made. Remembering her conversation with Shelly the previous night, she noted that again, here was a classic example of what they did and Todd was doing it now. He was putting his feelings away in his pocket and focusing on what needed to be done.

Bree wiggled out from under his arm and took his hands in hers instead. "Your offer means a lot to me and I want you to know that. I also want you to know that if I do need your help I will ask. But I first need to try to get through this on my own. I need to not hide what's really wrong away and face this head on. Does that make any sense?"

Todd nodded, "Sure, I can appreciate that. So, I'll give you the room to do what you have to as long as you shout when you need me. Deal?"

Bree took the hand he held out to her and shook it, lips curved in relief. "Deal," she affirmed.

"Now, the next confession," she declared.

"That sounds ominous," Todd stated, seriously.

"It's about the fight we had," Bree ventured. "No, nothing to worry about, I think," she rushed in when she caught him dragging a hand over his face.

"Do you think that now's the time to discuss that with what you're going through?" he questioned.

Bree tipped her head, "Yes."

"Okay," Todd waved a hand to illustrate his agreement, "what about that night?"

"I need to apologize to you," she began this new, difficult topic. "I realize now that I hadn't dealt with what we'd both gone through. More specifically, I hadn't dealt with me leaving Devil's Peak, my feelings about that, about us and then returning. It wasn't just sex that night, Todd. I panicked and used the sex, the lovemaking," Bree corrected, "as an excuse to not have to deal with the feelings I had from the past. The anger, the hurt, and the disappointment I felt in both of us. Talking with Shelly last night, I acknowledge that those feelings are normal but because I hadn't dealt with them, they were bottled up and after the kind of lovemaking we had, it kind of burst the bottle."

"What are you saying," Todd asked.

"I'm saying that I'm sorry," Bree professed. "I care for you too, Todd and always will and I'm sorry that I deliberately hurt you."

"Come here," Todd exclaimed and pulled her to his side. "Jeesh, you've had a hectic time!" He took a moment, rubbing his hand through his hair and over his face. Glancing at her, he noticed the pensive look in her eyes. "Since we're being honest with each other, I might as well add that I'm sorry, too. I was mad as hell at you. We'd had an amazing night together and then that fight just ruined it,

But, I said some pretty harsh things myself and I guess that I was trying to hurt you back. I do still get a twinge when I think of what I've missed in Amber's life and I do hurt when I think that you didn't trust me enough to come back for you. But in reality, it is what it is and no moping is going to change the circumstances. I knew that when I agreed to go ahead with this amicable co-parenting idea of yours. So, when I said what I did, I said it out of spite."

"Apology accepted," Bree said after a few minutes of contemplative silence, relief coursing through her and renewed hope that they could work things out.

"Ditto," Todd replied, playing on older, fonder memories.

For the first time since Bree had returned to Devil's Peak, the grins they shared were pure and honest.

Chapter 16

"Now you be a good girl," Bree leaned down and spoke to Amber, "and listen to Charlotte." Smiling at the gym's child-minder, Bree returned to the lobby to wait for Shelly who was getting changed. The gym wasn't very large, but considering it was one of the newer additions in town, as well as the only gym for miles, it had a bit of everything. Its only competition, the gym at The Lodge, was typically stocked with the basic equipment holiday makers sought out such as treadmill, step-machine, and a few basic weights.

It also meant that the place was packed with after-work fitness enthusiasts or people trying to get fitter, healthier, or thinner. Bree walked over to the large wall on the one side of the lobby that held a variety of notices, the classes held in the aerobics room and their services.

"Bree," Todd advanced towards her and called out in greeting. He looked like he'd just had a shower as his hair was all wet, a towel was draped around his neck, and he was carrying a zipped-up sports bag.

"Hi," Bree smiled back, focusing on his face and refusing to look at his long, muscular legs being shown off inadvertently in his shorts. "I didn't know that you come here."

"I have since it opened," he replied. "Since running the business interferes with the amount of time I can spend outdoors, I thought I better do something to maintain fitness."

"I've just joined myself," Bree answered. "Shelly's joined with me. I'm just waiting for her to get changed. Oh and Amber's in the children's area. She didn't want to join any of their exercise programs today. I think she's scoping out what happens here first before she decides what she wants to do. So for now she's happily making things in the craft area."

"That's okay," Todd nodded. "I'll pop by now before I leave and see what she's up to."

"Speaking of Amber," Bree ventured, "I've focused a lot on her this week. I wanted to show her that I was getting better. And one of the things I've started is a games night. It's basically a TV-free night where she and I play board games or Wii – quality time that's fun and does not require staring comatose at the television. My grandparents decided to join in and it actually turned out to be a blast. So, if you want to join us, you'd be welcome. We've dedicated every Wednesday night to it as it fits into Amber's homework and extra-mural time-table."

"That sounds good," Todd replied. "Thanks for the invitation. I'd like to join you."

"My pleasure," Bree smiled back at him.

"So, what do you have there?" He asked, pointing to the flyer she held in her hand.

Bree colored pink, wishing she'd hidden the darn thing away except that the baggy t-shirt and tights she wore didn't leave much room for stuffing things away in them – unless you put things in your sports bra and that was not something she was going to do. Maybe, though, it would've been preferable to do that than have him look at the flyer.

"Nothing much," she blushed harder, effectively mitigating the nonchalance she was trying to portray.

"Really?" Todd asked, disbelievingly. "Come on, Bree, give. I'll find out anyway and I've been coming here for a while so I know what's good and what to avoid. The special classes are expensive so my advice might save you money."

Bree sighed in resignation. When he got an idea into his head he was like a bulldog with a bone. She'd learned earlier on in their friendship, before they'd even started going out, to just give in – it was easier to say 'I told you so'.

He looked at the flyer in silence, his raised brows embarrassing her to no end. "Well?" Bree inquired. "What's your opinion?"

Todd looked back at her, "It's a waste of your money. You don't need post-pregnancy classes 'to hit those flabby areas you just can't get rid of'," he read from the flyer. "There's nothing flabby about you.

"You know how I feel about my tummy," Bree reminded him.

"Yes," Todd nodded, "and you know that I disagree." He stopped her retort with a show of his hand and went on, "Look, it's abdominal strengthening that you need."

Bree looked at him questioningly and Todd responded with a sheepish, guilt-laden grin. "I looked up the 'mummy tummy' as you called it after… you know…"

Bree nodded, waving a hand for him to continue. "Okay, before I explain what I found. I need to be clear that I think that there's nothing wrong with your body and that includes your tummy. I only looked it up because what you said made me curious – not because I agree with you."

"I get that Todd," Bree stated. How could she not have after he'd so sweetly convinced her? "The thing is that I still have issues with it and on this new journey I'm on, I'm doing something about the stuff

I don't like in my life or about myself. So, this," she shook the flyer in the air, "is for me. So, go on, tell me what you've found."

Todd searched her face and found genuine interest. Breathing a sigh of relief that his 'investigations' hadn't upset the apple cart again, he explained, "It seems that the plastic surgery information you read was accurate. There's nothing that can be done to bring the muscles back together again after having had a baby. But, you can strengthen them, which flattens and tones that area – not completely, but you'll see a difference. And the way to do it is pretty simple. In fact, I do them all the time. I could show you and save you the cash."

"Two things," Bree interjected, "while that," she waved a hand at the t-shirt covered six pack, "is hot on a guy. I personally don't want to be all muscular. And why do you want to do this?"

Todd shrugged, "We agreed last Saturday to work together and to try and forget the past right?" At Bree's nod of acquiescence, he continued. "I said that I'd help out if I could with what you're going through and I can with this, so why not?"

Bree recognized that he was waving a white flag and given the good place they were at, though not far from tentative, she felt urged to take him up on his offer. "Okay," she nodded, "if you promise that I won't become all muscular and sporting a six-pack, we have a deal."

"Bree," Todd replied, grinning, "A six pack is kinda hard to get and keep so there's no danger of that. So, you think they're hot, huh?"

Bree searched the floor for an invisible something and muttered, "You know they are, so stop."

Feeling oddly satisfied by the grudging compliment, he pointed his arm in the direction of a big, blue plastic mat towards the back of the weight-lifting area.

Bree put a hand on his arm to stop him. "I've got to go tell Shelly that I'm skipping this session with her."

"No need to," Todd responded. "I saw her go up the stairs and wave while we were talking. She must be going to the aerobics class and from the music coming from up there, they've started already. You sure you want to do this?"

"Sure," Bree answered. "I've never been big on exercise though, which you know, so I'm new at this. So be gentle okay?"

"With you," Todd looked down at her, making her insides melt, "always."

Oh boy, she thought, this should be interesting.

xxx

"So, what was up with you and Todd at the gym?" Shelly asked, sliding into the booth at the local diner. They hadn't been able to speak about it, after exercising as Bree had to get Amber home.

"And hello to you too, Shelly," Bree greeted, sarcastically.

"Oh never mind that," Shelly waved it away. "Spill."

"Todd's helping me work out," Bree shared. "He knows what physical insecurities I have, and when he saw the flyer I was holding, he offered to help out and save me some cash. So, once a week, when I'm not going to gym with you, he'll help me out. He's just being friendly after the chat the other day."

"I'm not sure that's all there is to it," Shelly offered.

Bree shrugged. "If there is more to it, then you know I'll be glad, but if not, then that's okay. We'll work things out. Our truce just seems a bit new to be jumping to conclusions or onto him just yet."

Shelly nodded, "Okay, you make a valid point. So, what's this meeting about?"

Shelly was referring to Bree calling her and their friends up to meet her at the diner. Bree had to drop Amber off at Todd's that afternoon for a play date and figured she'd use the opportunity to get together with some friends and pick their brain. She was touched that, despite the short notice she'd given them that morning, they'd all agreed to show up.

"Let's wait for everyone to sit down," Bree pointed at the diner's door where the rest of their friends were coming through.

Moments later with berry pie and coffees ordered, Bree explained the reason for the meeting. "Well first off, I realized, that I needed to see more of you guys."

"I agree," piped Kristine. "When you're married and you have kids, that can become the center of your life, as it should, but after going out with you guys the other night, I realized that I needed to get out a bit more – have some girl time."

The others bobbed their heads in agreement and Shelly suggested, "Seeing as we're all on the same page, why don't we agree that we do this the first Saturday afternoon of every month."

They smiled appreciatively at Shelly; she'd always been very managing. On the cheerleading squad, Bree'd had the ideas and Shelly helped figure out the details.

"Deal," they all said in unison and giggled liked the high school kids they had once been, feeling lighter and excited by the prospect of getting time off.

"Now, I want to pick your brains," Bree sat back and picked at her pie. "I spoke to Jack this morning at The Lodge about an idea. He wants to start using high school kids to work during the summer and on weekends as part of an internship program in hospitality management."

"What a lovely idea," Shelly clapped her hands in glee. "The DPC can help; maybe include it in one of the youth programs. And if not, we can certainly offer advice on what has worked and not worked for us."

Bree nodded, "And, I did tell him that. In fact, I gave him your number so expect a call."

"But, that's not why you want to pick our brains," Megan observed.

"No," Bree shook her head. "You know how I always enjoyed planning a party."

"Sure do," chirped Kristine, smiling wickedly and eliciting laughs from all around the table.

"Yes," Bree grinned, "we had those types of parties, too. But I used to love planning all sorts of parties – especially the kiddie ones."

"Oh," exclaimed Kelly, "I remember. You did the Halloween party for the kids for the DCP. That was adorable. You know, after that guacamole brain dip, I still haven't eaten any avocados to this day."

"And you did the princess and pirates pageant for the pre-school too," Alice reminded them.

"Yes," Bree bobbed her head, "those parties. Well when I was at The Lodge, I noticed that Jack had just installed a humungous jungle gym. It's huge, literally the size of a standard house. And he paid quite a large sum of money for it, because he ordered it from a company specializing in that type of thing. So, looking at it, I thought how much Amber would love it, and how nice it would be to have a party for her so that the kids could play on it. I realized that this was a gap in the market. So, why not throw parties there? When I mentioned it to Jack, he said that it was a great idea but that he didn't have the time or the staff capacity to go into such a venture. So, I asked him if I could give it a shot and do a demonstration as well as come up with a proposal. So, what do you think?"

"You're right about there being nothing like that in town," agreed Kristine. "I try to make Amanda's parties special but we always just end up having it at our house every year and it nearly always turns out to be a family meal with friends or a barbeque. Crazy Tom bought a few jumping castles in Fairbanks a few years back so we often get that too. Everyone in town basically does the same thing."

"She's right," agreed Kelly, "we try to make it exciting. Like for Steve's birthday, we got each boy a bug-hunting kit to keep them occupied and for something a bit different and then for Lacey we got a face-painting kit and my husband, Zach, dressed up as a clown." She broke into giggles, "That was hilarious, although the parents were more entertained by it than the kids."

After hearing more stories from the others on what was available in Devil's Peak and what they did, Bree felt that she had a better understanding of the gaps in the market. "You have no idea how much you've helped," Bree said thankfully, "I really appreciate it. So, now I have to figure out what to do for the proposal and demonstration. And, I have some ideas so I want to hit the shops before they close."

"Before you go," Alice stopped Bree, "Janet's birthday is next month, and like Kristine, I'm getting sick of throwing a summer barbeque every year. So, while you're thinking of ideas for the demonstration, you can think of Janet's party, too. That way, you can use the same décor and maybe even a similar theme."

"Thanks Alice," Bree leaned over and squeezed her friends' hand, no longer thinking of them as old high school friends, their bond had been reestablished. "I'd love to do Janet's party, but I'll let her choose her own theme – within your budget range of course. I'll call you after I finish the proposal and arrange to come over and chat with you."

"Sure," Alice nodded, "and bring Amber along. Janet's a bit younger, but she doesn't seem to think so, so I'm sure they'll be able to entertain each other."

Chapter 17

After breakfast and helping her gran clean the house the next morning, Bree sat down at the dining room table with a heap of material and all manner of crafty items – from fabric glue to glitter and beads, and a feather. She'd gone to the local craft and fabric store and had dipped into her savings, the previous afternoon to purchase it all. She'd worked on instinct, pulling from her dreams and her past experience and trusting that it would work out. The only guidelines she'd followed had been to ensure that she had enough pastel colors for girls, and bold colors for boys.

She'd also raided the attic and pulled out the décor items she'd used for the parties she'd organized before for the Devil's Peak Cares Association. As her gran was chairperson and said that none of it had been used since Bree last arranged a party for them, she didn't see any reason why Bree couldn't take it. Bree had felt obligated to the DPC nonetheless and had agreed to organize two parties a year for the DPC in lieu of payment.

Amber had slept over at Todd's the night before, so Bree used the quiet time to work. Cutting out material to the patterns, her mind buzzed with the possibilities each piece of fabric, and each tube of beads held.

"You look busy," Todd interrupted her, startling her.

"Hi," Bree looked up at him then got up and held her arms out to hug Amber.

"Good morning, honey," she kissed the top of Amber's head. "Did you have a good time?"

"Uh-huh," Amber replied. "We watched movies and dad taught me how to play cards so I can beat you on game night."

"I don't know about that," Bree said seriously, "I'm a mean hand at cards."

"Me too," Amber said, challengingly.

"I'm sure you are, honey," Bree laughed and pinched Amber's cheek. "Now go greet Grandpa and Grandma."

"Okay, I'm going to tell them that I'm going to beat them at cards," Amber replied, running off in excitement.

"What's all this?" asked Todd. "Are you redecorating?"

"Actually, I'm thinking of moving out of the farmhouse," Bree said deadpan, "and moving in with you."

"Huh?" Todd asked, doing a double-take. He cleared his throat and responded, "You caught me off guard – sorry. You're welcome to move in with me. I have three bedrooms and have been thinking of taking Amber to Fairbanks – with you of course," he quickly added," to get stuff to do up her room. Looks like you've got the girly stuff covered."

"I'm joking, Todd," Bree burst into laughter.

"What?" asked Todd, puzzled.

"I'm pulling your leg," Bree stated while thinking that she'd love to pull all his legs. "But, your response was sweet, thank you. And, I'd be happy to go with you and Amber to Fairbanks to find 'girly stuff' to decorate her room with."

"Jeesh, Bree," Todd swallowed, "since, you got your hair done, you've become feisty."

"I know," Bree's lips curved wickedly, slanting her blue ones up at him coyly. "Do you like it?"

Todd stared at the siren before him and recognized that the lust that shot straight through him did so a lot faster than usual. Fumbling around mentally for the right response, he forced a smile back at her, then thought stuff it. He took a risk and startled her in turn by planting a hot, fast kiss on her cherry reds. "Sure I like it," he grinned at her. "Confidence is a huge turn on."

He made a hasty retreat. Thinking that the quicker he got out of there, the less tempted he'd be to throw her amongst the glitter and feathers on the table and show her how much he liked it., "I've got to head back into town. I'll go say bye to Amber. See you tomorrow night at gym?"

"Sure," Bree croaked back, her hands flapping as she wove to his back. What was that?!

xxx

"We've brought dessert, kids, and extra hands," Shelly announced as she entered the dining room followed by Kristine, Alice, Megan, and Kelly and a brood of children.

Delighted by the company, Bree hugged each of them and made a point of kneeling down to hug and welcome each child. "Let me get Amber and my grandparents. They'll be thrilled to see you." Bree looked at the mess on the dining room table. "I was going to ask you to have a seat, but it's a bit of a mess."

"Don't you worry about that," Kristine waved Bree's sheepishly delivered apology away. "We didn't come to only socialize. We came to work."

"And who might this be?" Daniel's voice boomed with pleasure as he entered the room, Amber shyly walking behind him. "I see we have some helpers, Amber. I think that the garden fairy heard us and sent them. What do you think?"

Amber just stared wide-eyed, more at home with unfamiliar adults than children. "What's the garden fairy?" one of the little girls asked.

"Why, you don't know what a garden fairy is?" Daniel smiled down at the girl.

The children stared in fascination at the jovial, larger than life man and slowly shook their heads. Bree smiled broadly, she remembered that feeling when she was a child – her granddad had the ability to hook any child and fill their imaginations with tales from his Irish homeland. "Well, we better acquaint you then. Now, if you come with me, I'll show you the plants and vegetables that the garden fairy helps me grow. When Amber's grandma brings us cookies and juice, we can put little bits of it in the fairy garden Amber and I made for her. Then, if she feels like it – because the little people can be fickle – she might just show herself."

"What are little people," one of the boys asked as they tagged behind like children of the Pied Piper.

"I swear," Kristine declared, "if I could find what it is that your granddad has, Bree, and bottle it up, I could make billions!"

Bree laughed and looked around at her friends; ready to socialize and help her. An enormous feeling of belonging filled the part of her heart that could neither be filled by a man or by family and only by loving friends. And so, the loneliness, she realized, was on its way out the door. Instinctively reaching for her lips, she earnestly wished that the last part of her heart, the part that ached during intimate moments such as when she went to bed, woke up in the morning, or just wanted to cuddle, would be filled too.

xxx

A month later, Bree felt like her life was starting to get back on track. She'd seen Doctor Roz a few times and found that the therapy sessions were emotionally exhausting. But a few days after each session, when she'd had time to process what had been discussed, she felt better, as though she was making progress in healing. She had also been on the medication long enough that it had begun to take effect. At first she'd felt like she was cheating on her vow to get herself out of it, but chatting with Doctor Roz had helped her see that as a normal reaction and to see that the act of taking the medication was still her choice and by doing so, she was still in control of her journey.

All the positive steps she'd taken to improve her overall well-being were paying off too – in more ways than one. Improving her eating habits and the regular exercise with Shelly and Todd improved her energy levels and made her feel good about her body. It was still hard not to feel like she wanted to jump Todd's bones, but the more time she spent with him, without a variety of issues hanging over their heads, the more she felt as though she was getting to know him all over again. It was fascinating to observe how much both of them remained the same and how the seven years that they'd been apart had also changed them.

 Not only was she happier, but the other occupants of the Ramsay household were too. Her grandparents no longer slid worried looks her way. Amber was no longer concerned about her mother's health – something that Bree had confirmed after a long, honest chat with her daughter. The overall mood at the farmhouse had improved so much that it was a jovial place that called to you. Her friends and their kids had also been around again, having been more fascinated than expected, by Daniel's tales of fancy and skills with little ones and all things green.

All of this ran through Bree's mind as she sat on The Lodge's verandah sipping tea and enjoying the sight of her efforts. The gigantic plastic jungle gym was completely installed and next to it, under an especially erected marquis, were rows of charmingly bedecked children-sized tables and chairs, ready for the birthday princess.

Bree's proposal and demonstration to Jack had gone well. Though, Bree smiled to herself, she wasn't sure if Jack had listened to her very much, as he'd been fixated on the lovely Shelly. Shelly, being used to the appraisal that men gave her, had ruthlessly ignored the come-ons and puppy dog eyes that Jack had thrown her way. Either way, Bree had come out of the meeting with Jack agreeing to The Lodge providing Bree with exclusive rights to plan children's parties that were held there. It was a win-win situation really, regardless of whether or not Shelly's presence had clinched the deal. Jack could see the potential of offering a party service to longer staying guests or the odd families who brought their children on vacation for their birthday. More importantly, it would draw the local crowd to The Lodge during low tourism periods.

Thanks to Bree's impromptu inspection of the conference and wedding hall, there was also ample space to host adults and children for indoor parties during winter. The kids might not have access to the jungle gym outside then, but Bree had a couple of ideas up her sleeve.

Bree grinned as she continued to slowly savor her tea, recollecting the various experiments she was subjecting the Ramsay household and all its guests to. Oh, there'd been the expected cake-testing and requests for honest opinions of certain décor items, and with the boys and men at her disposal, they had proven invaluable in providing her with insight into what little boys would like for their birthday parties.

But, the most fun was had when, with the help of Amber's enthusiastic manipulations, she'd gotten Todd and her grandfather dressed up in a variety of home-sewn costumes. Not only were the men's personalities a poor fit for the costumes, but the costumes themselves were poorly constructed. But, Bree had persisted in her endeavors until Todd, the dear man, had walked into the farmhouse one day and unceremoniously dumped a couple of bags full of costumes, which he had rescued from a second-hand store in Fairbanks. The costumes were not in the best shape, but with the help of her gran, the DPC (on the promise of loaning it to them when they needed it and she wasn't using it) and her friends, they'd managed to get them into use-worthy shape.

For this party, Bree's second coordinated event, the theme was fairy princesses and the décor glittered and sparkled accordingly in various shades of pink and lavender. Heading towards her was the oldest fairy that would attend the party.

"Are you all set?" Bree asked Samantha, the high school student with a love for children and a bigger love for saving money for the prom. Samantha had stood out when Bree cast her eyes around for a child-minder amongst the teenagers in the DPC's youth programs. She was Bree's all-round helper and during the parties, the entertainer in whatever forms the theme required. For the first party, Samantha had donned a pirate costume without batting an eyelid and today, she looked splendid in a flowing fairy-costume with jewelry, make-up, and wings to match.

"Yes," replied Samantha. "I've got the list of games we agreed on and have practiced them all. Now, I'm just waiting for the guests. I'm ready."

"You'll be great and fun will be had by all," Bree encouraged.

"They're so adorable, that I'll definitely have fun," Samantha gushed.

"I'll be in tomorrow to pick up the tables and décor," Bree reminded her. "I've already checked with the kitchen and they're good to go. Jack's dedicated two waiters to serving drinks to the adults and laying out the food. Housekeeping will also pack up the party stuff and will store it until I come and pick it up. So, all you'll have to do is keep the kids busy."

"Should I help you with the cakes, quickly?" Samantha asked.

"Already sorted," replied Bree. "You can't see them because they're covered with a net. When the waiters bring the food out, they'll remove that too."

With everything in hand, Bree left The Lodge to pick Amber up from Todd's. The best thing about her new venture was that she got to do the planning and didn't have to stay for the hours it took to have a child's party. The fun had always been in the planning and preparation for her and with the set up that Jack had, she fortunately didn't need to see the execution to the end. That's why she'd been more than happy to agree to a forty - sixty split with him; it was a forty percent that she didn't have and she earned it doing something she enjoyed. What's more, involving Amber in the preparations had also given them hours of fun together.

Bree arrived at Todd's house, ready to pick up Amber and head on home to put her feet up while having a long, hot soak in the bath. She rapped on the door and got no reply. Leaning her ear against the door, she noted the silence, which was unusual for any environment that was occupied when Amber was awake. She looked at the driveway again and noted that Todd's truck was parked there. Going around the back, she was met with no sight or sound of life.

Starting to panic, Bree rapped on the back door and when no one answered her call, tried the handle. Finding it unlocked, she pushed it open. Again, the house was quiet - too quiet. "Hello," she called out, her voice echoing in the empty house. They'd definitely been here; Amber's toys were strewn around the living room. Picking them up as she went around, she fumbled for her cell phone with a free hand and dialed Todd's mobile. And, the darned thing rang in the kitchen.

"Bree, hi," Todd said, entering through the back door.

Bree yelped in surprise, having been completely engrossed in the ghastly scenarios a concerned mother's mind conjured up. "Todd! You scared the life out of me!"

"Sorry," Todd replied, chuckling and not sounding apologetic at all. "That's what you get for skulking around instead of sitting down and making yourself at home."

"I was not skulking around," Bree defended. "I came to pick up Amber."

"Oh, crap," Todd smacked his forehead. "I completely forgot."

"Where is Amber?" Bree narrowed her eyes at him.

"Relax," Todd warded her off, "she's just down the road with her friend from school. You remember Britney - Amber's height, brown hair, in the same class as her?"

"Oh," Bree said, and sank down into one of the kitchen chairs. "Thank goodness and yes, I know who Britney is."

"Oh, honey," Todd grinned, "you were worried." She was being an over-protective mother and it was adorable, if nonsensical.

"A bit," Bree lied, smiling sheepishly at him.

Todd let the obvious fib go. "So, Amber's not going to be ready for a while."

"Why not?" Bree asked then narrowed her eyes at him. "She got to you didn't she?"

"I have no idea what you mean," Todd replied, deadpan. "Amber gets a bit lonely with us adults and wanted to stay and watch movies with her friend. Then they were going to do girly things like play dolls or something. Britney's mom asked if it was okay and I said yes. It's good for her to play with her friends."

"Of course it is," Bree agreed, "and I'm glad you allowed her to play for a while. But, I don't for one minute believe that it was Britney's mom's idea."

When Todd opened his mouth to deny her accusation, Bree held up her hand and shook her head, "No, don't go there. You'll just dig yourself in deeper."

Todd's mouth flapped open a few times and then he shut it and shrugged. "So, Amber will be a few hours." At Bree's lifted brow, he specified, "Four hours because there's a full movie, cupcake baking, and tea-time with their dolls."

"Oh well," shrugged Bree, "like you said - it's good for her to play with her friends. As you pointed out, there aren't any nearby friends at the farm."

"If it's any consolation," Todd stated, "Amber promised to return the favor, so Britney's coming over here next Saturday afternoon to do the same - and I'll be getting the cupcakes ready-made. There's a big difference between a guy cooking and a guy baking cake."

Bree giggled at the image of Todd being thoroughly managed by two little girls, "Good luck with the store-bought cake idea. My suggestion - buy the cake mix in a box and ready-made frosting - easier than homemade but just as fun for the girls to make. And yes, that does help." Getting up from the chair, Bree hunted in her handbag for her phone again, "I'll call Shelly or one of the girls and see if I can pop around."

"What's wrong with here?" Todd asked.

"Excuse me?" Bree responded in surprise.

"There's no need for you to wait for Amber at someone else's home if you can just as easily wait here," Todd suggested.

"Okay, I'll stay," Bree accepted. "It'll give us a chance to catch up." He was testing their new, transparent friendship. Given that she'd wanted to stay, but didn't want to push things with him, his offer worked out well. With the exception of the one, searing kiss he'd given her a few weeks ago, their relationship had taken a completely platonic quality to it. Then again, they hadn't been alone until now.

"I've got a cherry pie that Amber and I picked up earlier and really good coffee. Can I get some for you?" Todd offered. "You look like you need a bit of sugar."

"I don't know about needing sugar," Bree smiled, "but I sure do want some. And your snobbish coffee would be great, thank you."

"Coming up,' Todd moved to the coffee machine, turned it on.

"Can I help?" Bree asked.

"Nope," Todd replied, "put your feet up. You were either really worried about Amber or you've had a busy day. You still look a bit pale."

"The day's been great. And, I was really worried about Amber," Bree confessed. "But, not because I don't trust you."

"No need to explain,' Todd waved the pending apology away, then placed a too large slice of cherry pie in front of her. "I'm not offended. It's your prerogative as a mother to worry about your child. I wish my own had worried about us for just a fraction of what you just felt."

"Oh, Todd, I'm sorry." Bree empathized. "Is it hard to see Amber and me together?"

"Not at all. It's a good thing. You're a good mother, Bree and Amber's a happy, loved child. I'm not sure how I'm doing yet as a dad. I'm taking it one step at time. I figured that if I go slowly that the mistakes I make will be easier to spot and rectify. But in terms of you and Amber, no, it's not hard. It gives me hope that because we're in this together, I'll do a better job of raising and protecting her than what I did for my brother and sister."

"That's bullshit Todd," Bree bit out, angry at him for his self-depreciating thoughts. "You did an excellent job with your siblings, which, by the way, wasn't your job to do in the first place. And, for what it's worth, you're a great father. So, you can stop the pity party right there."

Taken aback by the sudden outburst, Todd took his time and studied her expression; you could always tell what Bree was feeling by her expressions - she wore her heart on her face. "I know that. But, I don't always feel that way."

"Well get over it," Bree stated, still fuming. "For such a strong, intelligent man, you can have the most idiotic notions, and questioning your skills as a father is one of them. I could've understood this at the beginning, but not after seven months, not when you see our daughter happy, thriving, and loving spending time with you."

"Okay, point made," Todd gave in. Then with a glint in his eye, he teased, "Did I mention that you've become feisty since you've changed your hair color?"

"Indeed," Bree responded sardonically, taking a spoon of whipped cream, she tilted it upwards and flung it straight into his face. She waited just long enough to see his surprise, before getting up and running upstairs. Todd was fast on her heels, nearly catching her. Squealing, she side-stepped him and ran into the bathroom, locking it.

"Bree, come out," Todd ordered, "you're acting like a child."

Feeling like one, Bree stuck her tongue out at the door. "No way."

"I won't do anything," Todd promised. "I know you don't have clothes here."

"I am not going to fall for that," Bree declared.

"You can't stay in there forever," Todd stated, the obvious.

Bree realized that he was right, and that she hadn't quite thought this through - she should've first grabbed her bag, and then ran outside instead of into the bathroom. He'd be waiting for her at the door. Four hours wasn't that long, she lied to herself, and he wouldn't retaliate in front of Amber, so she'd wait for Amber to return and come out then.

After what seemed like ages, she felt as though she was going crazy. She didn't have her phone to keep her occupied or to call on someone to distract him and, she could only stare at and count the bathroom tiles so many times. Stuff invasion of privacy, she thought and opened the bathroom cabinet, inspecting the contents. It was decidedly unexciting - no hidden secrets to uncover. And, her idea of looking for products to maybe give her hair a good condition while waiting was not an option as the guy used a shampoo and conditioner in one! Visibly shuddering at what that would do to her own hair, Bree stopped, hearing movement downstairs. Perfect. She'd slip out of the bathroom, make her way outside and go, pay Britney's mom a visit.

Bree had just stepped foot on the landing, when Todd snuck up, jumped in front of her, and blasted her with a can of whipped cream. "Uurgh!" Bree groaned in frustration and lunged for him. Todd was laughing so hard that his attempts to dodge her failed, making it easy for her to tackle him. The surprise of landing on the living room rug stopped Todd's laughter. Caught in the childish freedom offered by the fun of the moment, Todd narrowed his eyes, contemplating as Bree grinned with wicked satisfaction, whilst straddling him and tossed handfuls of cream at his face, neck, and chest.

"Like that, do you?" Todd glared.

"Yep," Bree replied, rubbing cream into his t-shirt. "Okay Todd, you've had your fun and I've had mine. Truce?" she held her hand out to him.

"Truce," he agreed and shook her hand. Just as she was about to get up, he gripped her hand and brought her down onto his chest, rolling them both around so that he pinned her arms to her side and trapped her under his weight.

Bree was about to let a string of expletives out when she became aware of the heady sensation of huis attention on her. She glanced up and met his intent gaze, immediately cognizant of the warm, heavy feeling of muscle on top of her. The position that they were in was inadvertently yet explicitly sexual. Baby blues met warm brown eyes and the awareness progressed to the humming undercurrent of acknowledged desire. It would have been the perfect moment for a kiss - the all-consuming kind - but Todd ended the spell they were under. Holding out his hand to help her up, he threw a grin at her. "Yep, you're definitely feistier as a brunette," he teased.

Bree blinked, surprised by the abrupt change in atmosphere. Then she caught the scowl she almost let go of and buried it. Fine, she thought, I'll play along and responded, "You'd know, being one yourself." She satisfied her wicked thoughts with a slap to his behind before traipsing upstairs to clean up in the bathroom.

Chapter 18

"So, how was the movie?" Kristine asked, as they all settled down for gossip and giggles with drinks in hand. It was their monthly Saturday get together without the kids, and because Bree had to bake mountains of smurf cookies and cupcakes for a birthday party the following afternoon, they'd agreed to meet at the Ramsay farmhouse. The kids had grumbled about missing out on time with Daniel, but when their mothers had explained that Daniel and Moira would be visiting friends and that Amber would be at her dad's place, they'd acquiesced under the condition that they all got to go and help Daniel harvest the fall fruit from the greenhouse the next week.

Bree blushed, "How did you know about that? We only went last night."

"And your point is?" Shelly chirped, before sticking a blue cake-pop in her mouth. She pulled the cake-pop out, inspected it, and declared, "These are yummy. Where did you get the idea?"

"Google," Bree responded. "They're really just balls of cake mixed with frosting and covered with chocolate on a stick. Because the theme of tomorrow's party is, "The Smurfs," I had to use white chocolate, colored blue. I was a bit nervous that they might not come out right, so I'm really glad that you're enjoying them. And, there's more where that came from."

Shelly lifted a brow, "Sure, bring out the baked goods. We're happy to test anything. But," she wagged a finger at Bree, "that does not mean that you're allowed to change the subject. So you might as well get back to answering Kristine's question."

"It was great," Bree, replied, "We saw the new romantic comedy with…" At the sardonic looks from all of them, she laughed and gave them a bit more. "The movie was great and the company was better."

"Are you and Todd together again?" Megan inquired.

Bree shrugged, her face puzzled, "I have no idea. He calls often and not just to speak to Amber. Then again, it all started after I told him about Doctor Roz. Then, since that almost-kiss, he's started calling more often. We've shared a few meals, when I've popped around at his place, and Amber was playing with one of the neighbor's kids. And then, during our exercise session at gym the other night, he asked if I'd like to go and see a movie with him."

"Sounds like you're dating," offered Alice, getting nods from the rest of them.

"I'm not so sure," Bree said, shaking her head. "It's kind of like high school. I mean, we haven't even made it to first base since that one night."

"The one night where you told him that it's not all about sex?" Shelly questioned.

"Yes," Bree responded, grimacing at the recollection of the fight.

Shelly cocked her head, considered, and then spoke, "From what you've said, the fight was a mean one. And, you were quite vocal about sex complicating matters. If the guy really wants a shot at you, he's not going to go straight for the goal after you made your feelings so clear."

"But things have changed between us," Bree argued. "And, we don't talk about feelings or about us. We just kind of hang out and have fun together."

"Well, that's not a bad thing, hun," mentioned Megan. "You guys were always so intense around each other - like old souls who had found their long, lost loves, or other halves or something. It's not a bad thing to just relax and have fun. Heck, once you're married, sharing a mortgage, and many other bills, you don't get all that much time to just have fun. Sometimes I even have to pre-arrange when we're going to have sex."

"Really?" Bree asked, astonished.

"Really," Megan nodded. "It's not that we don't love each other or even want each other; life just gets in the way, sometimes of the more intimate part of a relationship, let alone the fun stuff like movies and dating."

"But that's just it," Bree interjected, "I don't know if we're dating. We don't talk about us in that way or at all really."

"Maybe you should ask him?" suggested Kristine. "What do you have to lose?"

"I've considered it," Bree agreed. "And if he doesn't make a move soon, I will ask him, but I'm still very weary to approach it with him. For the first time in ages, there's no drama with whatever is going on between us. Things feel natural, sexually frustrating, but I can live with that for a while longer. If it means that, we're building something here - if not for now, then for the future. I mean, he could just be being nice to me because of the depression. He did say that he would do what he could to support me. Maybe going out, having fun, the exercise thing, and the phone calls are his ways of showing that support."

"And, maybe I'm an eighteen year old cheerleader," Shelly challenged.

"Well, you were eighteen once and a cheerleader," Bree countered. "And, even though your tongue is blue from stuffing your face with those cake-pops, you, sadly, could still pass for eighteen."

"Yep," agreed Kristine, joining in on the teasing and giving Bree a helping hand out of the friendly interrogation. "Bree's right. You could pass for eighteen. I bet you even still wear the same bra size."

Shelly responded by throwing a cushion first at Kristine then at Bree. "You're right," she grinned, "my aim is still as good as when I was eighteen, too."

xxx

Fall was in full swing, Bree observed, relishing the crunch of the leaves underfoot as she walked along the main street of Devil's Peak. Already, the businesses were geared up for Halloween. Fake, plastic pumpkins, ghostly faces, and characters from scary myths and legends graced the windows of the businesses. Regardless of the type of business, each window display was using Halloween fever, a regular bug that bit during October, as a means of marketing their trade.

Bree passed by the toy shop, and despite her heavy load, was tempted to venture inside. Nearly an hour later, though it seemed like moments, she exited the shop with an even heavier load, having splurged some of the extra income she'd begun earning from the parties on yet more Halloween décor for Amber. One of the coolest things about being a parent, Bree thought, was the license to indulge your child and reap the same benefits of enjoying the treat without any guilt. So, really, the Halloween décor was for her too, not that she would admit that to anyone - including Amber.

Already the farmhouse looked like pumpkin-ville. Alaskans had the benefit of good soil and unusually long daylight hours from summer to fall, and the result sometimes were super-sized vegetables. With her grandfather's skill at anything growing out from the earth, they'd been able to supply nearly the entire population with pumpkins for the Halloween festivities. Of course, the Ramsay household and now Todd's place too, got the best of the bunch and about thrice as much as another indulgence to Amber. Although, Bree believed that her grandfather enjoyed her grandmother's pumpkin baked goods and carving the jack 'o lanterns as much as Amber did.

Todd, of course, had been included in the decorating and had entered into it with such eagerness that watching him Bree had felt moved. He'd never experienced any traditions celebrated when he was a child as there'd been no parental interest and no money. Now, that he had both a family and the financial resources, he seemed to be making up for lost time.

Bree was beginning to hope that this was the case with their relationship too. He continued to be singular in his attentions to her and being part of a small town, she knew that he wasn't dating anyone and in fact, hadn't dated anyone since she'd returned to Devil's Peak. But, the fact was, they were dating. Any intelligent human being would interpret the flowers she got on occasion 'just because', the movie and dinner dates, the impromptu lunches, and daily phone calls as such. The only thing missing was physical intimacy and now that she knew how great sex between them could be as adults, she felt like a starved dog staring at a bone every time they saw each other. She was starting to see Shelly's point about him being wary of going there with her due to what she'd said during 'the fight'. She was tempted to test that theory, but was still trying to figure out the best way to do it without outright seducing him and risking emotional rejection.

The Bree that had been depressed wouldn't have thought of Todd having genuine interest in her. And, Bree acknowledged, she'd always doubted, questioned his interest in her before being diagnosed with depression - as far back as when they dated in high school. Working with Doctor Roz, she'd unpacked her insecurities as well as her overly developed self-criticism and after months of therapy and a full prescription of anti-depressants, she could finally allow herself to feel good about the positive and negative in her. That also meant that she could allow herself to see how others truly cared about her and that included Todd.

Arriving at Todd's shop, Bree grinned at the 'ghoul-inspired' changes she saw through the window. Even the sign had been changed to read, "Scary Adventures." Again, it wasn't very imaginative, but to the type of clientele that Todd drew, it got the job done. When she entered the shop, Todd came forward to relieve her of the multitude of bags she carried.

"Is there anything left in town," he teased.

"I couldn't resist," Bree's lips curved in delight. "I will not go past the toy store again until after Halloween or better yet, until I need to do Christmas shopping. Besides, it's Amber's first Halloween in a proper house, with friends and family and well, I couldn't resist getting things I think she'd like."

"At this rate, we're going to have to build a shed to house all of it," Todd groaned.

"As if you'd mind," Bree scoffed. "Especially since you've spoilt her the most."

Todd grinned sheepishly, uttering denials that fell flat.

"Oh, and this is for you," Bree held out a bag. "Gran and I have begun bottling jams, pickles and fruit to fill the winter pantry. It's amazing that in summer we take it for granted and then in winter, when there's no fruit or fresh vegetables to be had, we'd die for a taste of them."

"It's in our nature as humans to forget. It's how we cope." replied Todd. "And, there's no need to die for anything. I can always get you what you want when we run the plane to Fairbanks."

"Thanks but I want Amber to fully experience Alaska and making do with what you have during our long winter is part of that. Besides, getting fruit in winter, even if it is coming from Fairbanks is super-expensive and a bit over-indulgent."

"With the exception of coffee, that's my philosophy too," Todd smiled appreciatively. "And speaking of coffee, do you have time for some?"

"Sure," Bree replied, amazed at how much had changed since the first time she set foot back in town and he'd asked her that same question. That day, she hadn't fully appreciated the gourmet coffee. Heck, she'd been a nervous wreck, worried about how he'd respond to the knowledge that he had a six year old daughter. In retrospect, she hadn't fully appreciated many things. Smiling to herself, Bree was glad that she had moved very far from that place.

"What's that smile about?" Todd asked, nosily.

In the past, her automatic response would've been something like, "Nothing much." Now, she felt secure enough to share. "I'm just thinking back to when I first sat in this kitchen and how far we've come. All of us - you and I have a great relationship as co-parents and friends, I couldn't ask for a closer bond between you and Amber, my relationship with my grandparents remains strong and I've even reformed old friendships."

Todd's eyes sparkled with sincere happiness for her. "That's really great to hear, Bree. I've noticed it too, but to hear you say it makes it more concrete. And, I'm very glad that you and I have resolved our differences. We're true friends again and I like it. I missed you all those years, so it's good to have you back home for good. So, I hope your happiness remains cast in stone." He raised his mug of coffee at her in salute.

Bree's lips curved at his sweetness, "Thank you. It means a lot to me that you feel that way. And may I return the sentiment. May your happiness, Todd, be real and true for you and may you have longevity and vitality." Bree clicked her mug against his.

"My pleasure," Todd responded. "And thank you."

"I have a confession to make," Todd admitted, "I've lured you here with the bribe of my superb coffee so that I could find out what we're doing for Halloween."

"I appreciate the coffee," Bree held up the mug. "But, you could've just asked or called. Frankly, I should've discussed this with you earlier, but I got a bit distracted with all the Halloween arrangements. I admit that I'm surprised that Amber hasn't spoken your ears off about the plans already."

"No problem," Todd shrugged, "my time is yours anyway. Amber did speak a lot. In fact she spoke so much that I'm kinda confused."

"The short version is that Amber is going trick or treating with the kids on your street. So, we'll get ready at your place. Then afterwards, the regular folk are coming over to the farmhouse for a party for the kids. We're also including the kids from the youth program, and of course, the entire bunch from Devil's Peak Cares will be there also."

"Sounds good," Todd nodded, looking thoughtful. "There's just one obstacle though."

"Oh?" Bree probed.

"I have to be back at my place by nine for a party," he clarified.

"Are you throwing a party?" Bree asked, waving her hand to stop his response. "No, don't worry. You're doing so much already by having us invade your home for the trick and treating. If you want to have a party, go ahead. That's okay. The main thing is that you see Amber and gush all over her princess costume."

"I'm delighted to host the trick or treating, as you put it, from my place," Todd stated. "But, I'll be coming to the farm, too. I'll just have to leave by eight."

Bree smiled broadly at him, "Thanks. That would be great and Amber would probably be close to asleep by then anyway. Who am I kidding?" Bree thought better of that wish. "Amber will be too fixated with her friends and high on candy to be concerned with any adult. Unfortunately, that includes us as her parents."

"I figured that," Todd returned. "But, I was hoping that you'd join me as my guest." When she looked at him in confusion, he clarified, "I was hoping that you'd come to my party."

Inside Bree was jumping up and down like a kid on a trampoline; she'd had some horrific Halloween imagery of Todd getting to up close and personal with a hot vamp-attired guest. With her being on the invitee list, at least she'd get her fair shot. Maintaining a semblance of outward calm, Bree responded with a broad smile, "I'd love that."

"Great," Todd grinned, looking as though he'd won the lottery. "We can leave the farm together."

Chapter 19

The Ramsay farm was a joyful, noisy center of activity as the Halloween party venue. Despite the late hour, the children were even more active than they'd been earlier when they'd been trick or treating. Given that that activity had been colored with eagerness and chatter, it wasn't a small feat to best it. Yet, little girls screeched as little boys teased with ghoulish stories and scary pranks, and some of them played and ran around the garden. In the living room, decorated to rival even the toy store, a horde of fascinated young faces listened attentively as Daniel embellished telling the tales of his homeland to them. Scary treats made of classics like 'witch finger' biscuits, 'mummy dogs' and 'ghosts in the graveyard' competed for tummy space with modern experiments such as brain jello and meatballs made to look like realistic looking eyeballs with sweet-chili sauce disguised as blood. And of course, there were loads and loads of candy in a variety of ghastly shapes and colors - the reason why the children were still running around as though it was early morning.

Bree found Amber and her grandmother and greeted them before moving on through the crowded dining room to wave at her grandfather. Worrying that Todd wouldn't find her; she decided to wait for him on the porch. Todd had excused himself earlier to fetch the food platters he'd ordered from The Lodge. Bree had raised a brow at that, thinking that he could just as well have helped himself to half the food at the farmhouse and he still wouldn't have made a dent in the supplies. She'd used the time though to change into a more adult Halloween, though decently covered, costume.

The gasps from the little girls playing in front of the house and the hoots from the little boys drew Bree's attention to the massive, beautiful white horse that entered the property. Squinting to get a better look, Bree noticed that the person riding the horse was dressed as a knight. Giggling at the reactions of the children and the difficulty the knight had in securing the horse while keeping the children at a safe distance, Bree decided to lend a hand. "Amber," she called out as loud as she could, "come quickly." Fortunately, Amber was in the dining room listening to Daniel's tales so she was close enough to hear her mom holler.

Amber knew that when her mom called to her in that excited tone that it was worth leaving whatever she'd been doing and run. "Wow," Amber exclaimed, flying down the stairs, very unlike a princess, to join her mother as she crossed the lawn. "That's a real prince and his horse."

Bree, giggled. Thank goodness, fairytales and knights in shining armor still existed in the minds of little girls. She'd believed in that fairytale too, but now she was ecstatic with a guy who flew a plane and made a living out of hosting Alaskan adventures. Come to think of it, Bree grinned, that sounded so much sexier.

"I think our prince is in trouble," Bree said to Amber. "It looks like the village children are swarming him, preventing him from venturing into the Ramsay castle."

Amber giggled, rolling her eyes for good measure. "Mom, we don't live in a castle."

But, Amber didn't say that the prince wasn't real, Bree thought, grinning at the selective attention of children. "Okay, well let's help the prince out anyway."

Hand in hand, Bree and Amber made their way to the Prince… Todd?

Todd, dressed as a knight, a prince to Amber, came towards them grinning widely and looking embarrassed. Amber, delighted, squealed, and ran to her father, jumping into his arms. Amber then placed a sweet kiss on his cheek and confessed, "I always knew you were a prince, Daddy."

"Of course," Todd puffed for her enjoyment, "how else could you be a princess?" After a number of appreciative kisses from Amber, Todd settled her on the ground and hand in hand with his daughter, approached Bree. "Our transportation awaits, milady."

Bree burst out laughing. When Todd continued to hold out his hand and remain silent, she realized that it wasn't a prank. "Really?" she checked.

Todd nodded before leaning down and kissing Amber goodnight. "I'll see you in the morning princess."

"Good night Prince Daddy," she curtsied before giggling and running to hug Bree. "Good night, Princess or Queen Mom." Then Amber dashed to the porch, laughing as though she were being tickled and chattering away about her daddy being a real prince to her great-grandparents.

By now, all the party guests, adults and children alike, were gathered outside or on the porch. Smiling with embarrassment, Bree took Todd's hand and allowed him to help her get on the horse. When he donned the knight's helmet, she couldn't help joining in the laughter as Todd expertly turned the horse around and rode away from the farm.

"Where did you get the horse?" Bree shouted to him, not sure if he could hear her through the helmet.

"The helmet's not real armor, so no need to shout," he replied laughing. "And, I loaned it from The Lodge," Todd replied.

"You've made Amber's night, Todd. Thank you."

"Did you enjoy it too?" he asked.

"It was adorable and cute," Bree replied. "It's definitely an experience I won't forget. I must say though that you definitely go all out for your parties."

"You have no idea," Todd shot back.

xxx

"What time is everyone arriving?" Bree inquired when they arrived at Todd's house.

"Everyone is nearly here," Todd responded, cryptically.

After Todd had secured the horse in the makeshift shed, he placed a call to The Lodge and asked them to bring his car back and fetch it in the morning. Bree saw that Todd had prepared the shed with hay, blankets, buckets of food and water so that it resembled a real stall.

Even though the ride from the farm to Todd's house was relatively short, Bree found that it took a few minutes until she felt as though she was walking normally again. Todd had been so gallant about the whole, sweet gesture that she didn't have the heart to tell him about it. He, on the other hand, having experience in riding horses, suffered no such side-effects.

"How did you manage to convince Jack to let you hire out his horse?" Bree wondered.

"That's between us," Todd teased. "Long story short, we're entering into a business agreement and I asked for a favor."

"Okay," Bree shrugged, Jack was rather generous but then again, Todd's skills in the outdoors were legendary in this part of Alaska and if Jack wanted to keep his guests safe while offering an adventure of a lifetime then Todd was the right one to help.

"Who put the lights on? And, why are we going around the front?' Bree asked.

"Because it's prettier," Todd explained.

He sure is talkative, Bree thought sarcastically. But he was also right. It did look ready for a Halloween party. Jack o' lanterns lined the path to the front door, where fake cobwebs, hollow bones and plastic spiders were ready to creep out eager trick or treaters. Tiny, plastic pumpkin tea-light holders were placed on the porch along the balustrade and a huge sign had been placed on the door, a boney finger pointing to the words, "Enter Please."

Expecting more of the same, Bree let out a gasp as she entered the house. Baffled, she looked at Todd, the house, and back again.

"Welcome to the party," Todd smiled down at her, delighting in her reaction.

"I don't understand," Bree whispered.

"Isn't it obvious?" Todd grinned. "This is for you, milady." He bowed and held out his hand to her.

Fascinated and touched, Bree took his hand and allowed him to lead her. When she entered the living room, it was even more beautiful. The hallway had been decorated with rows of glowing white candles, illuminating the space and casting a warm glow throughout the room. The glow from dozens of candles accentuated the colors of the profusion of flowers placed on every surface in the living room. Bree had always loved country flowers, preferring them to the more predictable rose and the more colorful and unusual, the better. The room held every country flower she'd ever seen and colored the room in hues of bright blues, pinks, yellows, and every color imaginable on a flower.

In the middle of the room, space had been created for a small two-seater table, which was draped with a long, white tablecloth on which stood a tall simple vase with a few sprigs of flowers. Wine glasses and an ice-filled bucket with a bottle of champagne stood sentinel, flanked the vase.

"I couldn't give you the flower-filled meadow you deserve," Todd said seating her, in all her witchy regalia, at the table. "So, I thought I'd create one for you."

Taking off the pointy black hat, she looked at him in the chair that he'd pulled up next to her. The feel of her hand in his, the room, and the thought and preparation it had taken to create this masterpiece, left her breathless and in a mild state of shock.

Todd grinned, he'd never seen her speechless before and he was going to take full advantage of it. "When we had 'the fight'," Todd began.

"No, please don't go there," Bree requested.

Todd shook his head, "I want to mention it so we can wipe it away for good. Let me explain please?" When she nodded, he continued, "When we had that argument," he amended, "you said that you want and deserve a man who will want to be with you, look for you when you're not around, cherish you, and love you."

Bree bit her lip and nodded. Taking a breath, Todd declared, "You were right to ask for it and I was wrong to think that we could have a marriage of convenience. You see, such a marriage between us wouldn't work."

At her sharp intake of breath, he smiled gently and carried on. "It wouldn't work the way I foresaw it then, because I hadn't fully realized how much I love you."

Bree couldn't speak because what she was feeling was so overwhelmingly wonderful. The shock slowly wore off and she started to regain her breath, excitement, relief, joy, and most of all the love she felt for him and felt from him flooded her senses.

"This isn't coming out of nowhere, Bree," he confessed. "After you told me about the depression, I did a lot of thinking and went to see Doctor Roz myself."

"And of course, as it's confidential, no one knew," Bree interjected.

"Yes," Todd agreed. "After I'd completed the therapy, I paid a visit to my mom's grave and then travelled to Ketchikan to visit my dad's grave too. The therapy made me realize that I needed to forgive them before I could move on. More importantly, because I hadn't forgiven them or myself, I wasn't able to forgive you for keeping Amber a secret from me."

"Oh Todd," Bree stroked the side of his face, mixed tears of sorrow and happiness sliding down her cheeks. "I'm so sorry for what I did."

"I know," Todd replied, taking her hand and kissing it. "And we already had this conversation and what I said then still stands true. I'm proud of how you've raised Amber and I'm happy that you're both in my life now. When you told me about the depression, I decided to go for therapy and work on the issues I had with my past. It wasn't an easy decision to make, but I figured that if you could do it and it was obviously helping you, then maybe I'd benefit from it too."

"Going to therapy was easy. It took a while longer for me to work around to forgiving my parents and myself. I realized very early on though that I still loved you. In fact, I loved you more because you've evolved from the vivacious, gorgeous girl I worshipped to a beautiful woman with a kind and generous soul that I adore, respect and love even more."

"So why did you wait so long?" Bree ventured. "I didn't know if you were being friendly or if you were interested in me."

"I wanted to journey into the next part of our relationship at my best, which to me meant that I needed to let go of the past with my parents. That took a bit of time. I also wanted to make sure that you were okay, and to give you the chance to focus on you and what you needed to do to work through what you were going through. So, I offered friendship first and then when that got too unbearable because it just wasn't enough, I decided to slowly woo you."

"Woo?" Bree raised a brow.

"I Googled romance ideas," Todd confessed, smiling sheepishly, "and they used that word often."

Giggling, Bree leaned in for a kiss. It was a soft, sweet kiss, drawn out to relish in the sensation of being kissed by someone who loved you completely. Gently pushing Bree away, Todd cleared his throat. "If we carry on doing that, I won't be able to stop, and I need to tell you something first."

"Okay," Bree sighed, playing with the armor he still had on, "although I'm happy with what you've said. I love you, you love me, and you want us to be a couple again. Now, can we get to the juicy parts please? My knight needs to rescue me from this sexual frustration I've been experiencing for longer than I care to remember."

Todd leaned in and clamped his lips on hers. Sighing in relief, Bree matched his passion and sank into the kiss. It was hot, brutal, and all-consuming. Then just as she ran her fingers through his hair to pull him closer, he pulled away.

He took a deep breath and let it out slowly. "I second you on the sexual frustration theory, but I do need to tell you something."

"Okay, Mr. Hunter, make it quick," Bree ordered, leaning back into her chair to put some distance between them before she grabbed him and changed his mind. He obviously had something important to say, she wanted to give him the opportunity, and whilst her hormones raged, she was in fact dying to know what it was.

"You said you loved me," he stated. "Why?"

Bree's lips curved slowly, savoring the emotions that flitted through her when she thought of the way she felt about him. "I love you because you're my best friend. You always were, and getting to know you again, I find that I respect and appreciate the changes that I see in you. I love how you've taken on the challenges that life's thrown your way and have risen way above them, more than anyone could've expected. I love how all that I believed that you were capable of, you've done and more. Not necessarily professionally, although that's impressive in and of itself, but in the way, you interact with others, the way you are generous, and tolerant. I love how I can act like a kid with you and how we laugh together. I love that our philosophies of life and parenting as well as our values match or complement each other's. I love how you are with Amber. Most of all, I love you just because. I can't explain it, but I feel as though there is a part of me missing when you're not near me and when you are, I feel drawn to you. I just plain love you, although I love you so much there's nothing plain about it really."

"Ditto," Todd replied. That one simple word echoed all that she said. Bree understood the significance. She understood that he was fulfilling her teenage dream of finding her version of love that Patrick Swayze's character in the movie, "Ghost" had for his wife. He'd remembered how she'd cried over the movie and lamented about how it must be the greatest love ever to have existed, even though it was fictional. He was telling her that their love was the real version of that and that their love was the greatest love. Mostly, he was telling her that he was willing to give her that love if she wished to accept it.

Todd stood up and walked to the nearby cabinet. Picking up a ring box, he returned to her and kneeled in front of her. He took a beautiful princess-cut diamond set in a simple, elegant white band of gold and held it up to her. The girl in Bree saw the ring and squealed in delight at the ring and the proposal but the woman in her reveled in the man who kneeled before her, professing his love for her.

"Bree Tanner Ramsay," Todd stated emotionally, seriously. "I promise to give you what you deserve, all that I am and all that I can be. I promise to love your heart, respect your mind, and worship your body. I promise to cherish our daughter and any other children you carry into our family. I promise to allow you to return those promises. With those promises meant from the depth of my being, will you fulfill my life and marry me?"

"Without any doubt in my heart and mind," Bree answered before throwing herself at him and sending them to the floor, the ring forgotten.

xxx

"Wait," Todd stopped their kiss.

"What now?" Bree grumbled.

"I love that you want me this much," Todd grinned.

"A big ego is not attractive in a man," Bree retorted.

"I can't help it," he replied. "With a beautiful woman like you wanting me this way, especially when I want you as much, how can I not have an enormous ego?"

Bree grinned, flipping her head to the side. "When did you become so smooth?" she asked, laughing at his expression of mock derision.

"When you became feisty," he responded, kissing her then getting up.

"What are you doing?" she asked puzzled, standing up too.

"Got it," he exclaimed, holding up the ring. He walked over to her and slipped it onto her finger. "This means that you and I belong to each other and I find that it's a heck of a turn on. It's to me what the hockey shirt is to you."

"That good huh?" Bree smiled wickedly at him.

"Oh, yes," Todd whispered, his lips touching her ear and sending shivers of anticipation through her. "I want to make love to you while all you are wearing is the scent of us and my ring on your finger."

"You know what I want?" Bree cocked her head to the side, studying him.

"If it has to do with the purpose of that ring or your delectable body then the answer is yes," Todd replied, kissing her neck as he spoke. The vibration of his voice against her throat, his breath caressing her skin and his tongue sending all rational thoughts away, Bree pulled back and stepped away.

"I have a final confession to make," she said, stepping away from him. Bree ignored his scowl and smiled with wicked anticipation. "I had a feeling that you wanted me but I wasn't sure." She shook her head, "I see that I was silly to be unsure."

She stepped out of her shoes and looked at him, allowing her gaze to travel down from his face, slowly over every inch of his body until she reached his crotch. "Yes, I was very silly to think so," she admitted, her gaze purposefully lingering on that spot. She began to unfasten the long row of buttons that went down the front of her knee-length, black witch's dress. "I was going to seduce you tonight," she confessed huskily.

"Well, you're doing it now," Todd bit out, fighting the urge to grab her and rip the darn thing off. The fact that she was standing in his house - their house - and that she loved him was enough of a turn on. That she was wearing his ring was driving him wild. But the confident, sexy seduction that she was subjecting him to, stole his breath away.

Bree didn't respond yet, but let her eyes rake over his body once more, as she strode towards him. "Remember how I told you that sex complicated things."

"Yes," he groaned. "And if you tell me that now, I swear that I won't be held accountable for my actions."

"Oh, I want you to be accountable," Bree unfastened the last button and held her dress closed with her one hand. "I want you to be accountable because you're going to make me scream and writhe and beg for your body. And, I promise to do the same," she touched his shoulder with her free hand and whispered, allowing her lips to graze his ear.

Todd hissed then pulled air in through his teeth very slowly to maintain control of the hot, hard punch of lust that hit him.

"Well," Bree continued with mock coyness, "I've decided that I like the complications that sex brings with it..." she trailed off before dropping her dress.

Bree had the satisfaction of seeing Todd's eyes popped as his stared at her, unmoving and with raw, debauched want. Using his momentary immobility to her advantage, she turned and made her way for the stairs. At the first step, she turned around and sweetly stated, though her eyes only spoke of heat, "I like the complications caused by sex, as long as it's sex with you." Then she let go of the seduction routine and ran up the stairs to their bedroom.

Todd shook his head to break the stupor. He loved that woman, he thought, before giving chase with a determined, sinful grin.

Prologue

The tiny Cessna, bearing the name, Hunter Couriers, glided through the Alaskan winter sky as it made its way from Fairbanks to Devil's Peak. Bree moaned at the jittery, jerky movements the plane made, willing herself not to vomit. Todd had decided to do the run as a treat for the family, which Amber had been only too willing to endorse. Because they'd both seemed so excited by the trip and insisted that it wouldn't be a family trip without her, Bree had caved in to the idea. Now, she cursed herself for doing so, although she had to admit that shopping for Christmas gifts in Fairbanks had been a lovely experience. She'd also managed to get ingredients for a Christmas dinner that she wouldn't have gotten in town and with Todd's brother and sister joining them this year, it was important to her that she pull out all the stops.

They'd turned it into a mini-vacation and had spent the weekend at a hotel. Amber had been thrilled at the treat, loving that she had her own room with a door leading directly into her parents. Amber had been more delighted though, to Todd's detriment when he got the bill, with the soft drinks stocked in the bar fridge. That would teach him a lesson for next time, Bree smirked to herself.

Thinking back to just two years ago, Bree marveled at the many changes coming home had brought. She remembered flying and feeling as terrified when she'd arrived with Amber, also during a snow-drenched winter. She recalled Amber's excitement about seeing her grandparents and her nervousness about meeting her father.

Just two years ago, Todd and she were at odds with each other. They had been two parents, circling each other over their child and not trusting or open to love. As a couple, they'd gone through much. But, they had worked through things and had now been married for nearly a year. Even more so, they'd each had to undertake personal journeys of letting go of the past and moving forward.

The plane shook and Bree bounced in her seat as they went through a spot of turbulence. Closing her eyes and breathing in deeply, she ignored Amber's excited chatter as she marveled at how high they were flying, how wonderful a pilot her father was and how tiny the web of rivers were below them.

"Are you okay, honey?" Todd interrupted Amber's description of the high mountains that they were flying above.

Bree opened her eyes and looked at his profile. My goodness but he's handsome, she thought. And he's such a good, wonderful man. Shaking her head at her sentimentality, she shouted back, "I'm okay. I just need to get home now."

Amber, sitting next to Bree, looked over in concern then shook her head. "It's fine Daddy, Mom doesn't like flying."

"I know sweetheart," Todd responded. "Will you hold her hand for me?"

"Uh-huh," Amber replied and slipped her little hand into Bree's, squeezing her mother's tightly.

Bree leaned over and kissed the top of Amber's head. Leaning back into the seat, she thought back again. When she'd returned to Devil's Peak, it was to confess to Todd that he had fathered a child and he'd been furious that he'd missed the first six years of her life. Surprisingly, he'd also been furious that he'd been robbed of the chance to be there for her during the pregnancy. Despite the feeling of nausea, Bree smiled. She wanted to get off the plane to be able to walk again on land. But, she also wanted to get off the plane so that she could experience one of many wonderful firsts yet to come with Todd and Amber. She'd do things right from the start this time, she smiled to herself. She'd tell them that their family would be one person larger in early spring.

As the plane descended, Bree thought of how she'd believed that she'd been coming home for good. Shaking her head at such utter nonsense, slanting her eyes first at Amber and then in Todd's direction, she realized that she'd come home for love.

About The Author

Aneesa Price writes romance and lives it with her university sweetheart and husband. After having surmounted the challenges of being in a bi-racial marriage in the newly democratic South Africa, she now attributes her marital bliss to purposefully added spice and passionately resolved differences. After living in a variety of cities in South Africa, the cosmopolitan city of Johannesburg is the playground that she enjoys with her husband and two daughters.

She writes to give her readers the gift of experiencing the new and fascinating, something she strives for herself when she explores new places, reads, cooks with her kids or goes picking for antiques with her husband.

She welcomes new connections.

Facebook Author Page

https://www.facebook.com/AneesaPriceSugarandSpice

Twitter

www.twitter.com/aneesaprice

Amazon Author Page

http://www.amazon.com/-/e/B008NA62CO

Facebook Fan Club

Aneesa Price's Fabulous Fan Club

https://www.facebook.com/groups/390755617667441

More By This Author

Coffin Girls, Elegantly Undead

(Book 1 of the Coffin Girls Series)

A Paranormal Romance by Aneesa Price

A sexy, female vampire with secrets. A sinfully-handsome witch prince on a mission. A formidable Vampire Council with something to hide.
A vampire descendent from the original Coffin Girls, Anais runs a successful event and wedding planning business from her majestic New Orleans plantation house. To the Vampire Council, she is seen as an exemplary hostess and household head of a misfit bunch of vampires. When Yves, her maker and head of the Vampire Council requests her assistance in hosting the mysterious, yet dashing Prince of Witches, Conall, she has no option but to accept. But Anais is the keeper of secrets; secrets that can kill. Protective of her family's undiscovered uniqueness, Anais is guarded, yet intrigued by the enigmatic witch prince.
Conall and Anais are drawn together when confronted with fatal encounters and an unimaginable destiny… if she's willing to accept it and fight.

Finding Promise

(Book 1 of the Promise Series)

A Small Town Contemporary Romance by Aneesa Price

A woman striving for independence.
A man with a charmed upbringing.
A small town filled with welcoming and quirky characters.
Caroline had led the life of a high society daughter and wife, one that was filled with soul-destroying emotional abuse. Upon the death of her

husband, she finds that she is financially incapable of supporting herself and flees New York without a plan or destination in mind. Her travels lead her to Promise, a small town on the New England coast.
Following instinct, she settles in Promise and begins to explore her new found independence and the pleasurable side of love with ruggedly handsome local, Luke Edwards. Her new-found contentment is shattered as past resurrects itself and she needs to find the courage to face it before she can truly re-build her life.

Ghosts and Lovers: First Confession

An Erotic Novella

By Aneesa Price

"I am female, I am a slut, and most days, I think I'm a loon too, but those are my secrets to keep except from you. … I ask you to play the role of a priest – nonjudgmental, understanding, and to atone me for my sins…" ~ Simone

Simone, the quintessential desperate housewife, is primarily absorbed on settling her family into their new home in the vibrant, metropolitan city of Johannesburg, South Africa. Unbeknownst to her, the greatest threat lurked not outside of the eight-foot walls and electric fencing but within the walls she seeks sanctuary. But the threat comes disguised as tantalizing pleasures of the most carnal nature that challenges her views of love, marriage and sex.
Can Simone resist and rescue her family from the evil she's let into their lives?
This is her first confession.

3470144R00114

Printed in Great Britain
by Amazon.co.uk, Ltd.,
Marston Gate.